First Frost

Women of Fossil Ridge Book Three
Lynne Gentry

TRAVEL LIGHT PRESS
FANTASY DRAMA ADVENTURE

Travel Light Press

DEDICATION

For my dear friends, Jana and Janet.
Tough women with no limits to their love.
I've always felt at home with you.

CHAPTER ONE

MOMMA DIED BEFORE THE bluebonnets went to seed.

I'll admit, my mother's passing came as a relief . . . at first. Not because I wanted my mother to die. No, quite the opposite. After a twenty-five-year cold war, we'd finally called a truce. We were in the beginning stages of rebuilding our relationship when the tiny cracks in Momma's cognitive abilities rapidly became uncrossable fissures. As my strong, brilliant, and talented mother transformed into a terrified and helpless child, I became more and more desperate to hang on to her. I searched for the best medical care, signed her up for the latest medications, made drastic changes to her diet, and spent hours trying to stimulate her mind.

Nothing stopped Alzheimer's wicked progression.

My mother's physician, Dr. Benjamin Ellis, an old friend I've always called Itty, reassures me that feeling a sense of relief is a normal reaction after caring for someone who is terminally ill. I don't need a doctor, even if he is also a well-meaning friend, to tell me that watching a loved one struggle to remember who she is, how to eat and, at the end, how to breathe is difficult.

But now that the temporary relief has given way to the grief, I'm the one struggling to catch my breath.

I grip the porch railing. The peeling paint is sticky with mid-August humidity. Overhead, end-of-season baby swallows poke their beaks over the edges of the muddy nests and squeal for their breakfast. I've ignored the poop-splattered porch planks long enough. Now that I'm no longer meeting the demands of Momma's care, I have the time to paint the porch, but I simply don't have the energy.

Losing Momma feels like I'm being held underwater, and the air is gone from my lungs. Benjamin assures me that I *will* surface. I'm counting on him to be right. I can't lose my job. My principal, Wilma Rayburn, has graciously allowed me to skip several summer in-service events. Tempting as it is to request a bit more time off, I can't.

This job doesn't pay well. Thankfully, the judge ruled that many women raise children on a teacher's salary. With careful money management, I should be able to do the same. With Winnie's astute legal representation, James and I reached a divorce settlement. To keep Aria out of a nasty, legal tug-of-war, I agreed to give my ex-husband custody of our bank account and all our shared properties. He agreed to give me full custody of Aria.

I definitely got the better deal.

Just how I'm going to pay for an advanced music education on the salary of a country school music teacher remains to be seen. I love my job. Teaching kids has fulfilled my dreams, the ones I had long before I assumed my sister's dreams. Becoming a lawyer was Charlotte's plan. Not mine. My foolish attempt to make up for my failure to save her had nearly killed me, and it almost destroyed any chance of ever reconciling with my mother. If coming home to take care of Momma has taught me anything, it's that I must never forget who I am again.

My gaze drifts to the rose garden. The New Dawn climbers have suffered under my lack of care, but the Butterfly Roses are more beautiful than I've ever seen them. The stunning mix of yellow, pink, and crimson blooms on the same stalk represents the changes that eventually come to all of us, Momma used to say. We're born yellow and bright, full of hope. Then as we mature, life's skirmishes pink us up. It's not until we've bled and learned from our suffering that we turn crimson . . . the most beautiful rose in the garden.

"Mom?" Aria steps out onto the porch. She has her Siamese cat Fig tucked under one arm and a cup of steaming Earl Grey in the other hand. The dark circles under my fourteen-year-old daughter's blue eyes are evidence that I'm not the only one having trouble sleeping. "Did you eat?"

I shake my head. "I'll grab a banana from the cafeteria."

"Yeah, but will you eat it?" She hands me the tea. "You're still losing weight." She seems to have matured from thirteen to thirty in a matter of weeks and that adds another layer of guilt to my shoulders.

I had to grow up way too fast after my sister died. I don't want my girl to miss out on what's left of her childhood. "Have I thanked you for helping me take such good care of your Nana?"

"Yeah, like a million times."

I tuck a blonde curl behind her ear. "It's time to let me look out for you now, okay?"

The screen door flies open.

Black and white teacup poodles yap around the feet of my overall-clad boarder, Ira Conner. "Goodness. Mercy. Hush."

The dogs obey the old man who has become such a comfort to me. Ira and his little dogs greet Aria and me every morning and every day after school. The old goat farmer is no longer able to do more than feed the chickens and tend Momma's parrot, but we love having a man around the house. He's both the grandfather Aria never knew and my father the way I always pictured him.

"Mornin', Ira." I shout over the barking dogs.

Ira waves us in. "Hurry." His eyes gleam bright as his bald head. "Bojangles is talking!"

Aria and I have to race to keep up with Ira's spry strides toward the kitchen.

Teeny, my other geriatric boarder, stands at the counter slicing apples. She's dressed in a lime green blouse and sports a giant tangerine bow clipped in her white hair. Rumor has it that I've taken in boarders to help defray expenses at Fossil Ridge. Teeny and Ira do not pay me a dime. They came here after they helped Momma escape from her assisted living facility. They live here because we've made them family.

"Sara was right." Teeny pushes her bow back into place. "This bird has become a regular chatterbox." She hands Aria an apple slice. "Like me, he has to be enticed."

I smile at Teeny's admission. When she and Momma first met at The Reserve, Teeny seldom spoke. Since becoming part of our family, she's talking more and more, a fact that warms my heart as much as it had cheered Momma.

"Go easy now, Aria," Ira coaches.

Aria lowers Fig to the floor then slowly approaches the ringneck parrot's cage. "Here, Bojangles." She eases the apple between the bars and holds it steady. "What does he say?" she asks Ira.

"Hang on," Ira says. "Give him a minute."

We all hold our breath and lean toward the cage.

Bojangles turns his head then inches along his perch bar. "Sweeeet Mo!" He snatches the apple slice and flutters to the opposite side of the cage.

"Did he just say Sweet Moses?" I ask Ira.

"We've been workin' on it for weeks." A grin splits Ira's wrinkled face. "Sara would have loved it."

The memory of Momma standing on the edge of the bluff and shouting her pet phrase at the top of her lungs brings tears. "Yes, yes she would have." I kiss Ira's cheek. "Thank you." I grab my satchel. "Sweet Moses, Ari. We've got to go. Nana would have had our hides for being late on the first day of school."

"Sweet Moses," Aria howls.

"Sweet Mo!" Bojangles echoes.

Spirits lifted, Aria and I rush out and climb into Momma's old car. Thanks to my neighbor Bo Tucker and his generous mechanical skills, the Escort is still running, which has saved me from adding a car payment to my slim budget.

"What about Teeny and Ira?" Aria asks as we bounce over the cattle guard.

"What about them?"

"Are you going to send them away?"

The question floors me. Aria knows it was my idea to invite Momma's friends to come live with us. "We couldn't have kept your Nana at home for as long as we did without Teeny and Ira's help." I press the gas, and we fly across the bridge that spans the Frio. "They've become so much more than Nana's friends. They're family."

Relief brightened Aria's face. "I was afraid you were planning to change things up since Nana . . . you know . . ."

"Died." I reach for her hand. "You can say the word, Ari. Because that's what happened. Nana died."

"I know, but saying it seems so . . . final."

Loss hangs between us heavy as wet jeans on a clothesline. Tempting as it is to let time dry the weight, I know better. Aria's heartbreak will grow heavier and heavier if I don't address how she's feeling.

I clear the lump in my throat. "When my sister died, my mother refused to use the word. She left my sister's room intact and acted like Charlotte was still away at college. Her denial and pretense made me very angry." Gravel pings the undercarriage. "It's okay to be sad that your grandmother is dead, Ari."

"Are you sad?"

"Yes, very."

She pondered my admission for a few minutes. "Are you going to sell Fossil Ridge?"

"Why would you think that?"

"Nana said she probably wouldn't even be cooled off good before you put her ranch on the market."

I don't know whether to laugh or cry. I thought Momma and I had cleared up any misperceptions we had about each other's motivations. Apparently not. "Good mothers do what's best for their kids. Education does not come cheap."

"Geez, Mom. How many times do I have to tell you? If you get me a horse, I don't have to go to Juilliard."

"We can't afford another mouth to feed." I crank the wheel and the Escort screeches onto the highway. "I gave up my dreams. I'm not about to let you give up yours."

CHAPTER TWO

THE LAST NOTES OF my vocal solo resonate in the empty church sanctuary. Fingers still on the keyboard, the words of the song continue to work on my heart.

"That was beautiful, Charlotte." At the sound of the deep bass voice, my eyes fly open. Itty's smiling at me from across the stage, his trumpet still in his grasp. "Breathtaking."

I shift on the keyboard stool. "Thanks."

Despite the maze of mics and instruments separating us, the doctor's brawny form takes up so much real estate on the small stage that I can almost feel him trying to catch his breath.

"Good work, guys." Itty's praise is intended for the whole band, but his gaze is still locked with mine. "Can't wait for Sunday."

The drummer, Arty Shaw, points a stick at our unlikely yet fearless leader. "Itty, I gotta hand it to you. Adding Charlotte to the band has definitely taken things up a notch." He slides his sticks into the back pocket of his overalls. "Don't let this one get away, Doc."

"Don't intend to." Itty's gaze is a laser burning through the excuses I've used to dismiss every dinner invitation he's offered since I became a free woman.

I break eye contact with Itty. "Thanks, Arty. I enjoy it." I quickly set to work gathering my iPad and purse. "See y'all Sunday." I push the stool under the keyboard and bolt toward the door.

"Charlotte!" Itty calls.

Crashing metal behind me is quickly followed by the high-pitched squeal of a toppled microphone.

I pivot in the aisle. Our brilliant band leader lies sprawled across the red carpet. Amplifier cords are tangled around his legs and sheet music flutters around his face.

Trying not to laugh, I ask, "You okay, Itty?"

"Yeah." His struggle to extricate himself from the snarl topples two more music stands. "Wait up."

"Smooth move, Doc," Arty laughs. "Reminds me of when you used to try to march and blow the tuba at the same time."

For some reason, the snickers don't set well with me. "Those cords are a hazard."

"Smart and talented." Arty begins to unwind the cords around Itty's ankles. "We gotta keep her, Doc." Arty offers Itty a hand up and with a sly grin says, "We'll lock up. You two go on now." He nods to where I'm leaning against a pew, iPad and purse clutched to my chest like a shield over my heart. Every man I'd ever known has disappointed me. I'm not bucking to sign up for another heartbreak.

Admirably unfazed by the teasing, Itty slaps Arty on the back. "Thanks, man."

The night is warm, heavy with the heat of late summer. I drop my iPad into my purse and hoist the bag over my shoulder. The heels I wore to school today click on the church steps. When I flew into the kitchen to grab a sandwich, I told Aria I didn't have time to change. Truth is that heels have always leveled the playing field for me. Made me feel more like someone who measures up. But something about walking beside this man who towers over me by ten inches makes me feel silly for thinking I need to try so hard with him.

Itty waits for me at the base of the stairs. "Arty's right, you know?"

"About your smooth moves?" I put one hand on Itty's shoulder, slip the slings from my feet, and wave the heels over his huge feet. "Maybe it's your shoes."

"Don't try to change the subject by discounting your musical ability, Charlotte. It's God-given."

"You're no musical slouch either, you know."

He offers a self-assured nod. For any other man this kind of confidence may have seemed cocky, but on Itty it's more of an admission of being comfortable in his own skin. "Ever wonder what would have happened if you'd followed your heart."

"Sure," I admit. "Don't you?"

"Not really." Peace radiates from his smile. "I enjoy practicing internal medicine in a one-horse town, fishing the Frio once in a while, and playing with our praise band."

"More than playing trumpet on major world stages?"

"Way more."

"Mind sharing your secret to contentment?"

"There are some good people in our little band, and there are some very sick people in our little town." At the edge of the sidewalk, he offers me the crook of his arm. "That gravel is going to hurt."

I thread my hand around the strength of his arm. "Momma was disappointed in my choice to become a lawyer." We go slowly as I pick my way over the pointed rocks. Itty begins whistling the tune I heard in the hospital after he treated my snakebite. The joy of it gives me the same comfort now that it did then. "I can't tell you how happy it made her when I came back and started teaching music."

Itty opens my car door. "Has it made you happy to be here?"

"Very." I free my hold on him and look up. "Hope I can stay."

His eyes narrow. "If you enjoy small-town living so much, why would you make a change?"

"Between the costs of keeping up the ranch and raising my daughter, I may not have a choice."

The disappointment on his face is a heart-stab confirmation of what I'd known but haven't wanted to admit since I came back to town. "We're just getting used to having you back," he says.

"We?"

"Me."

Itty loves me.

The realization stirs all sorts of emotions inside of me, including a guilty shame that I've given him false hope. After all the pain James put me through, I have no desire to start a new relationship.

Ever.

"The band's really coming along under your direction." I toss my purse onto the passenger seat of the Escort. "I gotta go."

Itty captures my arm. "I was thinking that you and I should take a stab at a duet."

"You deserve far better accompaniment than I'll ever be able to give." I rise on my tiptoes and kiss his cheek. "Good night, *friend*."

Dashing his hopes inflicts a hurt in his eyes I never intended. I turn away quickly, jump in Momma's old car, and peel from the parking lot.

I swore after Momma died that I was free of the past, but it requires every ounce of strength I have not to look back.

CHAPTER THREE

TEENY AND IRA HAVE joined me on the porch for our regular weekend attempt to stay out of Aria's way. Every Saturday morning, the older generation turns the dining room over to the hip young band my daughter has put together.

I love to hear Aria rocking the keys, but it's the smile her ever-expanding friend group brings to her face that really makes me hope we don't have to move.

Ira lowers his *Austin Statesman* to reveal two poodles curled on his lap. "The kids are sounding better." His voice rings with the pride of a grandfather.

"Ember's skill on the guitar improves every week." I shift the Siamese cat purring in my lap. "And I can't help but think that forcing Evan to sing in front of people will only help him when he re-auditions for NYU this fall."

Teeny looks up from the pile of hot pink hair ribbon in her lap. "That poor boy was so disappointed when he froze up at his last audition." Not only is Teeny talking more, but her spot-on observations would have pleased Momma to no end.

How I wish Momma was here to see the seeds of love and patience bloom in who was once a very lonely woman.

Tears spring to my eyes. It's these unexpected waves of grief that really get to me.

I pretend something's in my eye. "I think Corina was right to insist that her son spend a year working at the pharmacy and singing in as many little venues as she could book." I stroke Fig's tawny fur. "But I have to say, Ira, that once they added Brandon, the band really started to gel."

"Somethin' tells me my grandson ain't driving all the way from Austin every Saturday morning so he can play the drums." Ira's eyes twinkle. "That boy inherited his Pop's appreciation for blonde hair and blue eyes."

"Brandon and Aria?" I scoff. "She's not going to let a boy get in the way of her plans for Juilliard."

"Even these old eyes can see she's as sweet on him as he is on her." Ira snaps the paper and goes back to reading.

"Sweet." Teeny holds up a hot pink hairbow the size of a dinner plate and clips it into her hair. "Mail's here." She nods toward the cloud of dust following a multi-colored VW bug buzzing up the lane.

"What's Winnie doing up so early on a Saturday?" I rise from the porch swing and set Fig inside the screen door. Goodness and Mercy leap from Ira's lap and run to the edge of the porch to defend our property. "I better go see what's up."

I jog down the porch steps.

Winnie screeches to a halt. "Help me out of this sardine can, C."

My old college roommate, and better friend than I deserve, has been a little cranky these last few weeks. But I'm more than happy to cut her a little slack, in fact, I'm overjoyed. Afterall, it can't be easy to be forty-three and eight-and-a-half months pregnant. Winnie will be a great mother.

I pop the driver's door open. "When is Bo going to buy you a bigger car?"

Winnie's stomach is wedged tight against the steering wheel. "We've got a van on order." She hikes her broom skirt and throws out her left leg. Her ankles are twice as big as they were last Saturday when she stopped in for coffee. "Can you imagine me in a van?"

"Only if it's an old VW van that Bo lets you paint with your trademark psychedelic designs."

"Everyone's a comedian." She throws her right arm over her belly. "Give me a hand."

I grasp her puffy fingers and tug. "You're stuck tighter than a wine cork."

"I don't recall making fun of you when your body swelled with Aria."

"You were living in a Rwandan refugee camp, and didn't know I was pregnant."

"Still, Sara raised you better."

I tug but she remains wedged in tight. "You don't have to get out, you know. You could just pass my mail through the window."

"I have to pee," she huffs. "Besides, I want to be here when you open the letter from Juilliard."

"It came?"

A big smile adds to her pregnancy glow. "Got it in today's deliveries."

"What if she didn't get in?" I pull hard and Winnie pops out.

Winnie grabs my shoulders and steadies herself. "What if she did?"

"Good point."

"I seem to remember advising you *against* letting James off the financial hook."

"You know I didn't have a choice."

"We always have choices, my friend." Winnie stretches her T-shirt down over her big belly. "You let fear win that one."

"I couldn't let him have her," I say, putting an end to second-guessing my decision not to risk some crazy judge deciding in favor of my ex and his family's deep pockets. "Where's the letter?"

"Top of that box on the front seat."

I scoot around to the passenger side and snatch the creamy envelope from a pile of junk fliers. It's addressed to Miss Aria McCandless, but it's the return address that captures my attention. Juilliard, Office of Pre-College Admissions. Though the envelope is thin, it's heavy in my shaking hands. Aria's audition video either secured her a live audition spot in Juilliard's high school Saturday program or it didn't.

"I wish Momma was here."

"Me too." Winnie wraps an arm around my shoulder. "She worked really hard to help Aria earn her spot."

"You don't know . . ."

"No, we won't know until you open the letter."

"It's not addressed to me."

"I can hear that she's home. Call her out here!"

"Wait for me on the porch." I press the envelope into Winnie's hand. "No peeking."

I sprint toward the house. My daughter won't be able to hear me over Brandon's drums, so I slip inside and let the screen door slam behind me. I follow Ember and Evan's beautifully harmonized rendition of Lady Gaga and Bradley Cooper's *Shallow* to the dining room. Aria's tickling the keys, her eyes closed, and a serene smile on her face. She's so happy. Music is in her soul.

"Ari," I say when they finish. "That was great."

Her eyes fly open. "Geez, Mom," she huffs. "You promised you wouldn't try to coach us."

I raise my palms. "Not coaching."

She gives me her then-get-lost look, the one I seem to get more and more often since her grandmother died. I know she's trying to deal with her grief, but that she could pull away from me pings my maternal sixth sense.

"Could I talk to you for a sec, Ari?" I cock my head toward the door. "On the porch."

"Can it wait?"

"No."

"Geez, okay." Aria pushes back from the electronic keyboard I bought for the praise band. "Everybody take five," she tells her squad, as she likes to call them. "There are cookies in the kitchen. Y'all help yourselves."

Teeny is holding the envelope up to the sun and trying to make out the contents when we step out on the porch.

"Winnie," I chide. "What the heck?"

Winnie shrugs. "We're all excited."

"Open it, Aria." Teeny presses the envelope into Aria's hands before I have a chance to prepare my daughter for the possibility that she has not been granted a live audition.

Aria turns the letter in her hand. "It's from Juilliard."

"Looks that way," I try to sound certain that the world's most distinguished music faculty wouldn't dare reject my gifted girl, but inside I'm preparing to fly to New York and fight someone if they break her heart.

Aria drags her finger over embossed address on the envelope. "Should I open it now?"

"Yes!" Winnie catches my glare and makes a zipping motion across her lips. "Sorry, pregnancy brain." She waddles to the swing and sinks with a loudly pronounced groan.

Barn swallows swoop and squeal as Aria slowly runs her finger under the flap. My heart feels like it is going to explode. I study the perfect angles of my daughter's face as she reads the letter.

Nothing. No change. Nothing.

Aria quietly folds the letter. "Well, that's that, as Nana would say." She slides the letter back into the envelope. "I'm going to New York."

"What!!!!!" I don't know whether to scream or hug her, so I do both at the same time. "You little stinker. You scared me half to death."

"What does it say?" Teeny asks. "Read it out loud."

Aria's friends, alerted by all the screaming, spill out onto the porch with cookies in hand.

"What's going on?" Ember asks.

"Our Aria has been accepted to the most prestigious music program in the country." Teeny announces the news with the ease of a woman who finally has something to say.

Ember squeals and throws her arms around Aria's neck. When the two girls finish jumping around and celebrating, Brandon gives Aria a congratulatory hug that, I feel, lasts a hair too long. I see opportunity-envy flicker in Evan's eyes, but to his credit, he's quick to put out the flame and he, too, hugs Aria.

"Read the letter out loud," Teeny demands. "We want details."

Aria pulls the sheet of paper from the envelope. "Give me some space." Everyone, but me, backs up. I can't seem to let go. "Mom."

"Oh, right." I stutter-step backward and am saved from falling off the porch by the rickety railing. "I'm just so happy."

Aria's voice disappears into the dark clouds that suddenly roll in. Dollar signs thunder in my head. Anger rains down on me.

How I'm going to let my daughter go suddenly takes a back seat to a much more pressing fear. How on earth am I going to pay for Aria's dreams?

Chapter Four

COME SUNDAY MORNING, I have acquired a headache, but I'm no closer to securing a plan. I twist in front of Momma's bedroom mirror wondering if she'd stood here the day she had to tell me that they couldn't afford to send me to Juilliard. I study my image, hoping for a glimpse of my mother's reflection. Some sort of clue as to how she'd weathered my heartbreak.

"We're going to be late, Mom." Aria's standing at my bedroom door.

Worried that she caught me worrying, and aware of the irony of that, I chirp brightly, "Do you think my Wednesday skirt is too short for a Sunday morning church solo?"

"Geez, Mom. It covers your knees." Aria's gaze sweeps the clothes explosion covering the floor. "Nana would lose it if she saw what you've done to her room."

A few weeks after Momma died, I framed my move into her bedroom as an opportunity to give my teenager a little space. The excuse was a flimsy one. I moved in to Momma's room to feel close to the woman who'd kept me at arms-length for so many years.

"When did you start working with housekeeping?" I tease.

A brief smile crosses her lips but does not reach her eyes. "Just not sure I want things to change."

"Me neither," I say. "Are Ira and Teeny already in the car?"

"Yeah and they're burning up because the Escort's air conditioner is out of freon again."

"My head's pounding." I palm the wrinkles from my skirt. "Maybe I should stay home."

"There's no way you'd let me or any of your choir students bail on a performance. Besides, Ember and Evan are coming to hear you sing."

"Now I know I'm too sick to go."

"You can do this."

Pale lip gloss accents Aria's tanned face and sun-kissed blonde curls. The peach-colored sundress shows off more of the glowing skin that has come from allowing Aria and her friends to explore the river. My daughter is becoming a woman right before my eyes. All the stalling in the world won't stop the inevitable.

I tuck a curl behind her ear. "Who's going to keep track of me once you leave?"

To my surprise, she doesn't back away. "I can stay."

Her toothy fake grin and lifted eyebrows signaling her hope that I'll agree does surprise me.

I shake my head. "The live audition isn't until the end of February. You won't start the program until next fall. That gives us plenty of time to get used to the idea of spending the weekends apart." It would be hard enough to commit to giving up every Saturday for an entire school year if we lived in New York, but a commute from Texas means Aria and I must give up our weekends together . . . and just when we were really starting to enjoy the time.

"Juilliard's pre-college program is so expensive, Mom."

Call me chicken, but I'm not as tough as Momma. I can't destroy my daughter's dreams without exhausting every avenue, and I'm not going to let her shoot her dreams in the foot before we even try.

"According to my Google research—," I say.

"Wait, you're googling now?"

"You're not the only one who can work a phone, kiddo."

"Geez, Mom," she grins. "Proud of ya."

"Like I was saying," I continue although I know what I'm about to suggest increases the odds that I'm going to have to let her go before I'm ready. "Previous successful applicants recommend we schedule a private lesson with a piano faculty member *before* your audition. This allows the prospective student an early peek at the Juilliard environment, and it helps those on the selection committee put a name with the face on the resume. This means you'll have to work hard and fast because we're going to go during my next in-service."

"That's in a couple of weeks. How are we going to save the money to go to New York by then?"

Obviously, I have not concealed my financial angst as well as I'd like to believe. "If you'll promise to leave the financial arrangements up to me, I'll promise to leave the piano prep up to you." I hold out my hand. "Deal?"

She sighs as though she's disappointed, "Deal."

"This is what you want, right?"

"Sure, Mom."

Twenty minutes later, I'm walking the worn carpet of the sanctuary aisle. My worries about Aria's lack of excitement will have to wait. I have more pressing fears to face. The band is warming up.

Though I'm determined to make my daughter as proud of me as I am of her, I approach the stage with a mixture of apprehension and terror. I haven't sung a solo in public since I was in high school. But stage fright is not the main reason I'm fighting bat-sized butterflies in my stomach.

Itty is on the stage, whistling that enticing tune of his as he fiddles with the strings on his violin.

I'm expecting him to be a little frosty after my definitive dash to his romantic hopes. And though I have no intention of becoming romantically or emotionally attached to a man ever again, I could use a friend. Someone who can help me look at my options and make the right choices for Aria's future.

"Congrats, Charlotte." He sets his violin aside. Instead of the cold shoulder I deserve, his greeting shines with the same enthusiasm he gives the rest of the praise team. "Word on the street is that someone we all know, and love, is going to

Juilliard." He wraps me in a friendly embrace then quickly takes two steps back. "Good work, little momma. Miss Sara would be so proud."

Heat flushes my cheeks. "Winnie wasn't supposed to tell. Pregnancy has completely unhinged her lips."

"Actually, it was Evan Miller who spilled the beans."

"Evan?" My eyes dart to the open foyer doors where my daughter is laughing with the Miller kids.

"I called in a script Saturday afternoon and after he took the order, he said he thought I'd like to know, being a *friend* of the family and all." Itty leans in close. "Seems like securing a live audition spot for your daughter is something a *friend* would tell a *friend*, don't you think?"

I slide my iPad into the holder by the keyboard. "You don't know how many times I started to call."

"No," his eyes search mine. "I don't."

"I'm sorry, Itty."

"Charlotte." The pastor correctly interprets the flush on my face as embarrassment and artificially brightens to cover his interruption of my flimsy apology. "Just wanted you to know that I'm looking forward to your solo."

Reverend Seidman is new to Addisonville. I admire his youthful determination to bring this country church into the twenty-first century, but something about the way he quickly glances at Itty makes me suspect he's already gained the good doctor's confidence.

"Hope I don't disappoint," I say. "I'm fighting a little stage fright."

"Benjamin tells me we're blessed to have you."

"That so, *Benjamin?*" I tease in hopes of moving our relationship safely back into the *friend* sphere.

Now it's Itty's turn to blush. "Absolutely."

"I'm going to talk about unconditional love during the communion devo." The pastor's gaze darts between me and Itty. "Would you mind backing me with a little soft music, Charlotte?"

"Sure. Anything in particular?"

"Benjamin tells me you left a fantastic legal career to care for your mother. If anyone understands love, I believe it's you. I'm sure you'll make the perfect choice."

As the pastor bounces down the aisle, shaking hands with the early arrivals, Itty leans over and whispers to me, "Can't wait to hear *What a "Friend" We Have in Jesus.*" Itty air quotes the word *friend*.

His grin flies all over me. "I was thinking more in the lines of *When I Survey the Wondrous Cross.*"

"*Demands my soul, my life, my all.*" The song's lyric he throws back at me stops my heart. "I get it that you feel like everyone you've ever loved has left you, Charlotte. But what if I'm someone who won't?"

"You can't promise that."

"I can promise the Lord would have to call me home before I'd leave you." He turns and ambles back to his instruments.

Looking out over the audience, I spot Winnie and Bo Tucker in the mix of people heading toward their regular seats. That Winnie is here ten minutes before church starts speaks to the influence a man can have on a relationship.

I catch Winnie's eye and mouth *help*. She whispers something to Bo. He steps aside and she waddles to the stage, her hand on her protruding belly, a little scowl of pain on her face.

Seeing her struggle just to breathe makes any discomfort I feel about Itty's discussion of me with the new pastor, and who knows who else, seem kind of childish.

I swallow my frustration and meet her at the steps. "You look good, Win."

"For a beached whale with tree trunks for ankles." She rubs her lower back. "I don't know how long I can take these wooden pews this morning."

"Why don't you sit in the rocker in the nursery?"

"LaVera, God rest her soul, would turn over in her grave if we deserted the Tucker pew."

"Since when do you care what the establishment thinks?"

"Speaking of the establishment—," unable to bend, she motions me close. "Is there something going on between you and Itty?"

"Difference in musical interpretations."

"Hmmm." Her eyes narrow like they do when she's caught a witness in a lie, so she presses to see what else she can squeeze out of me. "Are you sure Aria still wants to go to Juilliard?"

"It's been her dream for as long as she can remember."

Suspicion raises Winnie's brows. "You're not the first mother who's tried to live vicariously through her child."

"Momma didn't push me toward Juilliard because she didn't get to go. She pushed me because she thought I had talent. No one was more disappointed when the money wasn't there than my mother."

"Speaking of Momma and money, how close are you to wrapping up her estate."

"Almost ready to go to probate."

"Are you sure you've found all the assets?"

"There wasn't much to find," I say quietly.

"At first glance." She leans in. "What if she has an unknown life insurance policy or stock portfolio or some mature CDs?"

"I didn't find anything like that in the stacks and stacks of papers I sorted through."

"What if she had a safety deposit box?"

I shake my head. "I checked her bank."

"Did you check her *daddy's* bank?"

I wince at the thought of walking into enemy territory. "Why would Momma leave anything in her father's bank? That man made it very clear that he wanted nothing to do with my mother or her daughters."

"What if she wasn't the one who did the leaving?" Winnie leans as close as her stomach will allow. "What if your grandfather regretted his decision to ex-communicate her? I heard he wasn't a bad man. In fact, Burl Addison, Sr. was loved in this town. What if he was too prideful to make it right, so he left her something to make up for his mistake? Something in a safety deposit box with your mother's name on it?"

"You need to lay off the incense," I lightly tap Winnie's belly. "Or have this baby before you lose all your brain cells."

"Burl, Jr. was the most likely executor of your grandfather's estate, and as such, he is bound by law to notify any and all of his father's beneficiaries."

My gaze skirts to countdown clock on the back wall. Only three minutes until I need to be back behind the keyboard. "Burl, Jr. wouldn't ruin his reputation over trying to cheat his sister."

"Exactly. That's why I think you owe it to yourself and to Aria to at least investigate the possibility of a safety deposit box in your mother's name. Burl, Jr.'s bank could be sitting on a fortune that belongs to your mother and, by law, now belongs to you." Winnie winces and grabs her back. "Ow!"

"Win, are you in labor?"

"No."

"How do you know? You've never had a baby before."

She dismisses my concern with a bristle. "I may not know a lot about being a mother, but I know I wouldn't let hard feelings keep my child out of Juilliard." Winnie holds up a palm to silence my rebuttal. "Save your arguments for Itty." Her broom skirt billows around her as she waddles to the second row.

Itty's giving me the sign to take my place for the start of the service. I'll have to apologize to Winnie later for not appreciating her advice or her amplified hormonal state.

By the time the band finishes up the second song of the worship set, the fear in my stomach has swelled to the size of Winnie's baby bump.

My eyes ignore my commitment to distance myself from the infuriating doctor-slash-bandleader-slash-marginal-friend. The second I visually seek him out, our gazes collide. I don't know how long he's been looking at me, but from the tiny smile pushing at the edges of his beard, he's not surprised I've turned to him for support.

Without breaking our eye contact, Itty places his trumpet in its stand, picks up his violin, then nods for me to start the intro to Fernando Ortega's *Give Me Jesus*.

Fingers trembling above the keyboard, I keep my gaze glued on the lack of condemnation in his eyes and take courage in his belief that I can do this.

Itty and I are several measures into the intro, his exquisite support priming my courage. I take a deep breath and open my mouth.

"Ahhh!" Winnie slaps her hands on the pew in front of her and half-stands. "My water just broke!" Her cry drowns out my blurted note.

Bo leaps to his feet and sends his songbook crashing to the floor. "It's too soon, Winifred."

"Explain that to our baby." Winnie's knuckles whiten on the pew.

Murmurs ripple through the congregation. I'm frozen at the piano.

"Okay. Don't panic." Bo hooks Winnie's arm. "The bug's right outside the front door."

Winnie pulls free of her husband. "I can't fold myself into that tin can." Her clenched teeth shred Bo's suggestion. "This baby is coming NOW!"

"Everybody, just stay calm." Itty morphs from musician to doctor before my very eyes. Completely unruffled, he carefully lays his violin inside a velvet-lined case then clears the stage in two commanding steps. "Breathe, Winnie." He moves Bo out of his way and wraps his big hand around her wrist, then looks at his watch. "I'd rather we did this at the hospital."

I snap free of my shock. "Somebody call 9-1-1." I scramble out from behind the keyboard. "Hang on, Win."

Bo's rakes his hands through his hair. "She's not due for two more weeks."

Itty gently lowers Winnie back onto her pew. "I'm more concerned that she's high risk."

Wide-eyed congregants leave their seats and push to the front of the sanctuary like rubberneckers on a freeway.

"Can we give her some room, folks?" Bo's rebuke presses them back. He turns and claps a hand on Itty's shoulder. "You got to stop her labor, Doc."

"Not without some drugs."

"Charlotte!" Winnie screams. "Get these two idiots out of my face."

"Win." I kneel beside my friend. Fear for her has accelerated the adrenaline created by my pre-performance jitters. It takes considerable effort for me to match Itty's calm. "Itty's right. You need to be in a hospital."

"This kid is coming," Winnie puffs. "Somebody better be ready to catch him." She looks up from her panting. "Move it, people!"

"Aria," Itty calls.

Ember and Aria push through the crowd.

"Sweet Moses!" Aria rears back in alarm when she sees Winnie's wet skirt. "Is she bleeding to death?"

"No." Itty tosses Aria his keys. "You girls run to my truck and get the medical bag I keep behind the seat."

Aria quickly regains her composure. "You got it, Doc."

Itty looks at me. "Charlotte, go to the baptistry dressing room and bring me every clean towel you can find."

"On it." I sprint over the cords strewn across the stage and bust through the backstage door.

My palm drags the wall for the light switch. Unsuccessful, I'm forced to start up the dark, narrow steps guided only by the smell of chlorine. When I reach the top, I locate the little door that leads to a tiny dressing room. Luckily, it's not locked. The light switch is just inside the door. Clean white towels are stacked on a metal rack. I grab them all, and as a last thought, I snatch all the baptismal robes.

By the time I dash back into the sanctuary, Pastor Seidman has cleared out the place. Bo has lifted Winnie by her under arms. Itty has a grip on Winnie's ankles.

"On three let's move her to the aisle," Itty directs.

"No!" Winnie screams.

I hold out my stash. "I've got towels."

"Spread them over the carpet," Itty orders.

In seconds, I've made make-shift pallet for Winnie. "What else can I do?"

"Roll up a couple of those robes to prop behind her lower back," Itty says as he and Bo carefully place Winnie on the floor. "Bo, you seat yourself behind your wife. Make yourself into a human chair so that she can brace herself against your chest."

I squat beside Winnie and help her lean forward to give Bo enough room to swing his legs into place as carefully as possible.

Bo settles into position. "I'm set."

Stuffing baptismal robes between them, I say, "It's going to be okay, Win."

"No wonder you only had one kid, C. This hurts." She's trying to make light of the situation, but I can see the fear in her eyes. "What if I'm too old?"

"Too late to worry about that." My glance darts to Itty. "You've got a great doctor."

Aria and Ember race in with Itty's medical bag.

"Here you go, Doc." Aria deposits it within Itty's reach. "You gonna let her have a baby right here on the carpet? That'll leave a stain they'll never get out."

I can't believe how much Aria sounds like Momma. "Aria, why don't you and Ember wait outside the auditorium?"

"Geez, Mom, you always make me miss all the fun." She grabs her friend's arm. "Come on, Em."

"Whoa, girls," Itty says. "Until the paramedics get here, it's all hands-on-deck." He opens his medical bag. "Aria, go to the kitchen. Fill the biggest bowl you can find with hot water. Stop by the teacher's supply closet and find a ball of string or yarn. Ember, go to the nursery. Bring us any clean sheets and blankets."

The girls scatter.

Itty lifts a bottle of hand sanitizer from his bag. He squirts a big glob into his palm. "Do the same, Charlotte." He tosses the bottle to me. "Rub it up to your elbows."

I nod and get to work scrubbing in.

Winnie's alternating between breathing and panting, "I need to push."

Itty gently bends Winnie's knees then he takes a professional peek beneath her broom skirt. "Not until the baby's crowned." He lays a pair of surgical scissors on a clean towel. "Wait until I give you the go-ahead, understand?"

Sweat beads Winnie's brow. She nods.

Bo kisses the top of his wife's head and offers both hands for her to hold. "You got this, my love."

I'm contemplating their total reliance upon each other when Aria and Ember return with the supplies.

"Okay, everything's ready on my end." Itty rubs his hands together. "If this little fellow is ready on his end, you'll being holding him after a couple of good pushes." He peeks again beneath Winnie's damp skirt. "He's crowned."

"Fold her skirt back, please," Itty tells me. When I've finished my task, Itty cups his hand for the catching of the little Tucker. "Winnie, I want you to grab hold of Bo's hands and push at my command."

Winnie complies. Itty alternates between whistling his calming tune and calmly talking Winnie through the optimal moments to bear down. I find myself breathing and straining along with my friend giving her all for this new life.

Winnie lets up and falls back against Bo. "I'm done."

"You're doing great," Itty coaxes. "One more good push, Winnie, and he's all yours."

Bo, Aria, Ember, and Itty are all watching Winnie, but I'm watching Itty. He's completely unruffled. Entirely focused. And captivatingly compassionate.

In my book, his loving and gentle care of an elderly woman with a disintegrating mind had already proved him an amazing doctor. His joy at bringing a child into the world proves him a man far too amazing for me to keep pretending I don't admire everything about him.

Sirens sound in the distance.

"Hang on, Aunt Win," Aria says. "The ambulance is almost here."

"Too late. He's here." The baby slips into Itty's hands.

"Sweet Moses!" Aria gasps.

"This boy has a mind of his own," Itty says as he lays him on a clean towel.

"Just like his mother," I say.

Itty's not looking at the baby. He's looking at me, his eyes wet with emotions. Through my own tears, I wonder if Itty wishes this were his baby. It strikes me as totally unfair that he's not a father because he would make an excellent one.

Heat flushes my cheeks. "He's perfect, Win," I whisper.

"Perfection if I ever saw it." Itty's gaze burns a hole in my heart. "Well worth the risk."

Over the slippery body of a tiny new life, my excuses for never loving again drain away.

CHAPTER FIVE

ARIA AND EMBER BEG me to stay at the hospital. Evan convinces the girls to let him drive them home. The progress the Miller boy has made from a difficult, unmotivated student to a kind and ambitious young man surprises me almost as much as Winnie becoming a mother after all these years. I guess I have Momma to thank for both changes. She was the one whose wise counsel helped me crack Evan's shell, and my never-lacking-an-opinion mother was the one who finally blessed Bo Tucker's choice of a wife.

Itty and Bo flank either side of Winnie's hospital bed. The precious bundle in her arms has been nursed, Apgar-tested, weighed, bathed, and declared perfect by the entire congregation, all of whom have filed in and out all day to offer their congratulations.

"I think you've got a baseball pitcher, Bo." Itty wraps his stethoscope around his neck.

Bo hasn't quit smiling since the baby arrived. "I've got a glove for him at the house."

"Whether Truman becomes a baseball player like his father will be totally up to him." Winnie kisses the tiny fist clinging to her finger. "Parental expectations, whether real or perceived, are detrimental."

Winnie's statement is not meant to embarrass Bo. This wisdom nugget is directed at me and the expectations she believes I've put on my own daughter.

I change the subject. "Truman Tucker has a nice ring to it."

"Bo and I found each other when we'd given up hope of ever having someone of our own to love, let alone a family." Winnie glows. "Truman is proof love only needs the smallest ray of hope to flourish."

"Thanks to both of you for all you did today," Bo says.

"You two make a good team," Winnie adds. "Sorry I ruined your duet this morning."

"It was supposed to be a solo," I say.

"Really?" Winnie strokes Truman's chubby cheeks. "Because what we did get to hear was the perfect marriage of piano and violin. That's a duet, right?"

"I think Truman's untimely arrival was an answer to my prayers," I laugh. "My solo was Itty's idea. Not mine."

"There's always next Sunday." Itty's tone is so intimate it feels like we're the only two people in the room.

Heat flushes my cheeks. "I don't think so."

"I think Winnie's on to something," Itty says to me. "A duet would take the pressure off you." He moves toward me, his eyes sparkling with the dare. "Spread the anxiety around."

"That's an offer you shouldn't refuse, C." Winnie yawns. "But she will, Itty. Too risky."

I drag my gaze from Itty and force myself to concentrate on my friend. "I think somebody needs a nap."

"Yeah," Itty agrees, taking my elbow. "We should go and let Winnie sleep while she can." Itty's touch is a fire that shoots through me. "Charlotte tells me that once you bring a baby home you never have a good night's rest again."

"I didn't say that," I argue.

"No, but the dark circles under your eyes tell me you've not slept much since Aria got news of her live audition."

Winnie cuddles her baby close. "Doc's a smart one, C."

"Valedictorian of our class," Itty jokes.

"And humble," I add.

"Humility is overrated." Winnie hands Truman off to her husband. "Support his head, Beauregard." She settles into the nest of pillows. Exhaustion presses in on her joy. "From where I sit, you two make a good team." She closes her eyes. "Almost as good as me and Beauregard," she murmurs dreamily.

I kiss Winnie's forehead. "Sleep well, my friend."

In the hall, Itty and I stand inches apart, his hand still supporting my elbow. Neither of us make a move toward the elevator. It's as if the tremendous amount of love and happiness we've witnessed today holds us captive.

"We do make a good team." Itty's voice is thick with the same flood of emotions I'm struggling to control.

I raise my gaze to his. His eyes are welcoming pools.

I want to throw my arms around his neck and tell him how impressed I am with how he handled a serious medical emergency in the middle of a church sanctuary aisle. I want to tell him that there's no way I would have even joined the church band, let alone considered singing a solo, if he hadn't believed in the power of music to restore my brokenness. I want to say that I've longed to share my burdens since I was eighteen but have been hurt so badly by men that I'm terrified to trust again. And scariest of all, I want to say that since anyone I've ever loved has been taken from me, I'm afraid to love again.

Instead, I stay rooted to the floor, arms safely tucked against my side, and try for a light-hearted tone, something that won't betray this lump in my throat. "Maybe we should take our act on the road."

"Duets and Deliveries."

"Has a ring to it," I agree. "You can whistle, and I'll learn to yodel."

"I'd like to hear you yodel."

A squeaky wheel on a blood pressure machine a nurse is pushing down the hall interrupts the comfortable pause.

I fill in the gap with, "How are you going to get home, Itty? You left your truck at the church."

Itty strokes his beard. "I was so focused on getting Winnie and Truman to the hospital I didn't even think about my truck when I hopped in the ambulance."

"I followed you in Momma's car, so I've got the Escort," I say. "I'm happy to drop you off."

"You followed me?"

"The ambulance."

The same pleased grin he'd given me when I sought his support before my solo tugs at his lips. "You hungry?"

"Starving."

"Sonic's the only thing open this time of night."

"I seem to remember you promised me a limeade if I'd join the band."

"And I never break a promise." He takes my hand. "Never."

CHAPTER SIX

OVER HAMBURGERS, FRIES, AND cherry limeades Itty and I laugh about how Momma would've reacted to Winnie delivering a baby on the floor of a church sanctuary.

"This is not a commune, Winifred." I scare myself at how precisely I can mimic my mother's voice.

Itty dips a fry in spicy mustard. "Your mother had her opinions."

"It's scary how Aria sounds just like her, don't you think?"

He waves the yellow-tipped fry at me. "DNA is strong. Sometimes, you act like your mother."

"No, I don't."

"Never wrong, unwilling to ask for help, and relationship adverse."

"Momma had friends. Teeny. Ira. LaVera."

Itty raises his fry. "I stand corrected."

"After LaVera died, Momma was so loyal to her old friend that she felt it necessary to act like she wasn't pleased when Bo announced his engagement to Winnie. In truth, Momma was thrilled to see LaVera's only child so happy. But to keep from admitting that she might have been wrong about Winnie, Momma said, 'LaVera would turn over in her grave if she knew a hippy was moving into her house.'" I look at Itty and he's trying not to laugh while he chews. "Okay, you're right. Momma didn't like to admit she was wrong, but that doesn't mean I'm like that?"

"Sara's stubborn insistence that I was wrong about her Alzheimer's diagnosis kept her alive well past medical expectations." Itty dips another fry in mustard. "I'll never forget the day I came down the hall of my office and overheard your mother standing up for you with my receptionist."

"You heard her tell Corina she was a spiteful little thing in third grade and that she still was?"

"Yep."

"I know Corina understood Momma's illness, but I'm still mortified. Corina didn't deserve that."

"Maybe not." Itty stuffs the fry in his mouth. "But the stern talking-to Miss Sara gave Corina made my receptionist a lot more cognizant of all my patients."

"Better a talking-to than the ruler I guess."

"Miss Sara rapped my knuckles a time or two and look how great I turned out."

It feels so good to laugh with someone whose roots run deep inside the fabric of my life. Itty may tease, but I don't have to explain or defend the woman that was my mother because I know that he loved her, too.

I dab the corners of my mouth and admit, "Momma was one hard-headed woman." I lower the napkin. "And then suddenly she wasn't." The pain of watching my mother lose interest in everything from music to arguing lodges in my throat. I can barely whisper, "When she became cooperative and strangely quiet, she became someone I didn't know." An unexpected tear trickles down my cheek. "I'd give anything to hear her sharp-edged opinions again." I swipe the warm wet streak. "I hate that my mother and I allowed pride to keep us apart for so many years."

The lights inside the Sonic suddenly go dark. The owner and two employees step out into the sticky air. Itty and I sit in silence as the drive-in's evening shift locks up and says their goodbyes. The manager sees us staring at him through the windshield. He waves goodnight but leaves us parked in the glow of the flickering neon sign.

For some strange reason, tears come in abundance. They drip hot down my cheeks. I blink but can't stop them.

Itty fishes around in the paper sack filled with condiments and retrieves a fresh napkin. "Here."

I shake my head, disgusted at myself. "I thought my tears were finished."

Itty reaches over the sack. His big hand cups my face with the same tenderness I'd witnessed as he shepherded a new life into the world only a few hours ago. "Grief doesn't play by the rules." The pad of his thumb slides across my cheek, careful and slow, as if warming the fragile skin of a newborn. "Charlotte, you sacrificed a lot to save your mother's life." His touch sinks beneath my tough exterior and heats the ice around my heart.

"No, Itty." If he kisses me now, I will not be able to stop kissing him back. "Momma saved me," I whisper.

He leans closer. "For what?"

"For you." I lift my gaze to his. "Momma said I'd be a fool to pass up a man with good teeth and a respectable job."

A pleased chuckle reaches to Itty's eyes. "Did she tell you that I've been in love with you my whole life?" He's so close now I can feel his breath mingle with mine.

"Every chance she got."

When our lips touch it's not the sensation of skin on skin I feel. Instead, music buzzes from my head to my toes. The melody is supported by the perfect union of forte piano and mellow brass. A beautiful concert sweeping along measure by delicate measure, a collaboration that ends far too soon.

Itty lifts his lips from mine with the finesse one might expect from an expert trumpet player known for sustaining a perfect note far beyond human endurance.

I'm the one in need of breath. Oxygen hits my brain and rational thinking takes over. "Itty," I push away. "I'm sorry, I can't do this—"

"Life is short, Charlotte. There are no guarantees."

"Nobody knows that better than me."

Itty sits back in the passenger seat. "Maybe it's time you tell your heart."

"I have responsibilities."

"Investing in your personal well-being is not selfish." He stuffs hamburger wrappers in the bag between us. "In fact, allowing yourself to risk some happiness is the best way to ensure that you'll actually have something to give those who are depending on you."

I don't know what bugs me more, that this man knows me so well or that I could get used to kisses laced with a kick of spicy mustard.

CHAPTER SEVEN

THE HOUSE IS DARK and quiet by the time I slip inside the screen door. I'm relieved that Aria, Teeny, and Ira have been in bed for hours. I don't want to explain my flushed cheeks or conflicted thoughts.

My finger traces the tingle of Itty's thick beard on my lips. There's no way I'm going to be able to sleep until I sort the ramifications of having the medicine-slash-music man admit that he loves me and wants us to spend our lives together. He was gracious when I told him that Aria has to be my priority. But I could tell my neutralizing response stung a little.

My pell-mell dive into marriage with James McCandless centered around one consideration: getting back at Momma. It can be argued that I paid for that foolish choice. In spades. What I find harder to forgive myself for is the realization that I was not the only one hurt. My daughter may suffer for my failure to consider the consequences of revenge for the rest of her life.

If watching Momma struggle to rectify her mistakes has taught me anything, it is to learn from previous missteps. Every choice I make from here on out must be made with Aria's future well-being in mind. Following my heart today when it could adversely affect Aria tomorrow is not an option.

I slip my shoes off, pad to the kitchen, and pull the string above the sink.

Yellow light startles Bojangles. "Sweet Mo." He flutters to the opposite of his cage. "Sweet Mo."

"Shhh," I whisper. "If you keep my inability to sleep between us, I'll give you a pear slice. Deal?"

He shoots me a dirty look. "Sweet Mo."

I grab a pear from the basket and a knife from the chopping block. "Momma and her blasted birds." I slide the fruit through the bars. "Just because you can talk, doesn't mean you should." I wiggle the slice and Bojangles waddles close. "Sometimes it's best to keep your mouth shut and pray about something for a few days." A chuckle escapes me. "Lord help me. I'm starting to sound like my mother."

While I'm waiting on Momma's parrot to comply, I notice a large white envelope on the table. It's addressed to the parents of Aria McCandless and it's from the Financial Aid Office at Juilliard. "This should bring me back down to earth."

I flick the pear slice into the empty birdseed feeder, pull out a chair at the kitchen table, then open the envelope.

The numbers are sinking boulders in my gut. Tuition for the pre-college-Saturday-only program is over $10,000 a year. This does not include a year's-worth of weekend flights to and from New York, a modest food budget, occasional hotel rooms, or taxi fares. There's no way I can stretch my $40,000-a-year teacher salary to cover both Aria's dream and the needs of this ranch.

I scan the letter again. Near the bottom of the page, in tiny print, is a heading entitled: *Financial Aid and Scholarships*. I read over the eligibility requirements and application process. Even if Aria happens to win one of the coveted full-tuition scholarships offered, I'd be hard-pressed to cover the other expenses.

My head drops in my hands.

Bojangles pecks at the bell on his swing. I lift my head. Two beady black eyes consider me from behind gold bars.

"Any suggestions?" I should feel foolish for talking to a bird, but instead I hear Winnie's words in my head. What I *should* feel foolish for is letting James off the financial hook for his daughter's education.

"Sweet Mo," Bojangles squawks, head cocked to the side.

"Why would Momma . . . wait a minute." What Winnie mentioned at church about the possibility that my mother could have yet undiscovered assets in my grandfather's bank hits me with a new and pressing urgency. "Bojangles, you're brilliant."

I blow the parrot a kiss, pull out my phone, and text my principal.

Sorry for the short notice, but I have estate business to attend in the morning. I'll schedule a sub.

CHAPTER EIGHT

JUILLIARD HAS A 6.4% acceptance rate. The pre-college admission competition is so tight that most piano students aren't even offered a live audition opportunity. That Aria has secured a live slot means someone, other than her mother and grandmother, believes a girl with her talent belongs at the most prestigious music conservatory in the country. Aria deserves the shot Momma and I never got.

I've rehearsed these facts all the way to town. By the time I park Momma's Escort in front of her father's bank, I'm regretting taking Winnie's advice. The odds of my grandfather leaving hidden treasure in my mother's name are about as great as Momma leaving me some kind of written blessing.

I'm familiar with those odds because before I moved into Momma's bedroom, I tore the place apart searching for a letter she might have left me. I looked under her bed. I dug through all the unused presents I'd given her over the years. I even emptied her underwear drawer. I found prescriptions that had expired in 1987. I found a little box containing a pecan with 1968 written on the shell. A bank book with each payment made on the ranch carefully recorded was tucked into her bedside table. Under the bed, I discovered a small plastic tub filled with mementos of her life. Wrapped in tissue paper was the little lacy dress both my sister and I wore home from the hospital. Beneath this yellowed frock, she'd carefully placed her marriage certificate, the birth certificates for me and my sister, and the death certificates for my sister and father. These were the things of value to Momma. But there was not a single message of love. To me or anyone.

A quick stop at the County Clerk's office before I came on to the bank confirmed what I'd suspected. My mother's brother, Burl Addison, Jr. was the executor of my grandfather's will. As such, my uncle will know if his father left my mother anything in a safety deposit box.

Asking my mother's brother about the possibility of a secret bank box without accusing him of stealing from my mother is going to be tricky. I don't know my uncle. I've only met him once, and that was years ago after a football game. Our family had accidentally run into him and his wife Virginia on our way through the exit. The exchange between my father and Burl had been friendly enough, but Momma gave him an icy stare that froze any further conversation.

I take a deep breath and trudge up the steps of the three-story bank building with my mother's family name etched in the Hill Country stone. I remember Caroline and I letting our curiosity about our grandfather get the best of us once. We slipped away from Momma while she was at the drug store and skipped across the street. Standing on our tiptoes, we held on to the shiny brass door handles and pressed our noses to the lead glass. We were so disappointed to discover that everything inside was distorted beyond sorting.

After my grandfather's death, the heavy brass-plated doors were replaced with modern, solid-glass doors in an effort to give the illusion of fiduciary transparency. Hopefully, Uncle Burl has moved on from whatever separated him and Momma.

Stepping inside, my hopes of progress are dashed by the musty smell of ink, paper, and old fixtures. Worn oak floors creak beneath my heels as I make my way toward a woman sitting behind a mahogany desk my grandfather probably purchased for cheap when he took a huge risk and opened this banking business in the late 1930s.

The attractive woman looks up from her computer screen. "May I help you?"

I shift the purse strap cutting into my shoulder. "I'd like to speak to the bank president."

"Do you have an appointment with Mr. Addison?"

"No."

"Would you like to make one?"

I glance to the rear of the building. A large plate glass window gives me visual access to a bald man sitting behind a huge desk. "My business with Mr. Addison will only take a minute."

The woman, Gina Calvert, according to her nameplate, eyes me suspiciously, "I'll call him." She picks up the phone. "Your name, and the nature of your inquiry?"

"McCandless. I'm an attorney seeking the assets of a deceased client."

She points to an upholstered chair. "Have a seat, Mrs. McCandless."

"Miss," I correct.

"Miss McCandless."

She presses a phone button, lowers her head, and speaks softly into the receiver. "He'll see you." She cocks her head toward the president's office. "Go on back."

By the time I walk the length of the bank, my uncle has come out from behind his desk. He's straightening his jacket and plastering on a smile.

"Miss McCandless, I'm . . ."

"I know who you are, Uncle Burl."

His face scrunches in confusion. "Uncle?"

"I'm Charlotte. Sara's youngest daughter."

"Oh." He pulls at the hem of his jacket and lifts his chin. "I'd heard you'd come home to care for Sara."

"Have you heard she died?"

Sadness wipes the smile from his face. "I have. I'm sorry for your loss."

"Not staying in contact with Momma was your loss too, Uncle Burl."

"My sister could be difficult."

"I know that better than anyone, but I'm not here to add to your guilt." I help myself to one of two chairs in front of his desk. "I'm simply on a mission to wrap up Momma's estate."

"And how do my sister's affairs concern me?"

My nod to the other chair is my signal to him that I will not be intimidated. Once he's seated, I withdraw some photocopies from my purse. "According to the County Clerk, you were the executor of your father's estate, correct?"

He ignores the papers I'm holding out. "Yes."

"As such, you were legally obligated to notify all beneficiaries named in the will."

"Now see here—"

"I'm not accusing you of failing in your legal duties, Uncle. I'm simply asking for your help."

"What kind of help?"

I slip the papers back into my purse. "Is there any possibility that my grand-father left anything addressed to my mother? Perhaps a safety deposit box in her name? A letter? Anything?"

Uncle Burl's shoulders slump, as if he carries a great weight. "I never did approve of my father's decision to cut off Sara," he says quietly. "In fact, for years, Virginia and I managed to sneak out to the ranch and join Sara and Martin for an occasional swim or picnic. Not long after Virginia and I married, the doctor told us we were never going to have children of our own. Every opportunity to enjoy Sara's daughters was a gift we treasured. When you were about two, Virginia and I took your parents a sack of pecans we'd gathered from our trees. We had a glorious day at the river. But when Virginia and I returned home, Father was waiting on our porch."

The importance of the pecan I found hit me hard. "Was that 1968?"

He snaps from his memory. "I suppose. Yes. Probably about then. Why?"

"I found a pecan labeled with that date in Momma's things."

"I loved my sister." Uncle Burl's eyes glistened. "For years, I've kicked myself for allowing Father to keep me from Sara."

"And exactly how did he do that?"

Uncle Burl's hands wave over the bank. "He forced me to choose between making a living for my wife or befriending my sister and the son-in-law my father despised." My uncle shakes his head. "A decision I will always regret."

Compassion surges through me. Who am I to point fingers at anyone unwilling to knock down the walls of long-held misunderstandings or unfortunate life choices?

I reach for his hand. "Uncle Burl, do you think your father might have regretted his decision as well?"

"Not as far as I know."

"Can we at least look and see if there is a safety deposit box in Momma's name?"

"The thought never occurred to me, but absolutely."

We spend the next thirty minutes with our heads together, going over computer records and handwritten ledgers that precede my grandfather's passing.

Nothing. No attempt to reconcile on this side of death.

"I'm so sorry, Charlotte." Uncle Burl takes my hand. "If things are tough at the ranch, let me help."

"This is something I've got to figure out but thank you." I rise on my tiptoes and kiss his cheek. "Uncle Burl, I'd love for my daughter to get to know you and Aunt Virginia."

His face brightens. "We'd like that. A lot."

I leave without adding a dime to my bank balance, and yet, I feel flush with happiness.

Momma would never have thought it possible to restore the brother she needed worse than I need cold hard cash.

CHAPTER NINE

I PACE THE PORCH, noting that Aria's little dining-room band sounds better this weekend than it did last Saturday.

Winnie, who is still on maternity leave from the postal service, has come for a visit. Sitting on the porch swing, she looks up from the dark-haired little boy sleeping in her arms. "Why are you so anxious, C?"

"I have a lot on my mind." I've told Winnie there is no secret stash of money in Uncle Burl's bank. I haven't told her, or anyone, that I've talked to Sam Sparks about selling the ranch. "Aria's private lesson has been scheduled for two weeks from today."

Winnie cocks her head toward the open window. "You sure classical training is the kind of music Aria wants?"

"Garage bands are a teenage phase," I say. "Juilliard offers a viable career in music."

"Didn't you and Itty have a little jazz band in his garage?"

"Yes and look where that got me."

"Playing with him again and happier than you've ever been?"

"Confused and ready to break up with him and his praise band." The moment I spew out this withheld detail, I feel foolish for allowing myself to fall prey to Winnie's excellent cross-examination skills. Next thing you know, I'll be telling her about Sam Sparks.

The enlightened grin she gets when she knows she has a reluctant witness over a barrel tugs at her lips. "You kissed Itty, didn't you?"

"You should never have left law, Win." I drop beside her on the swing. "Yes," I admit. "I kissed the infamous, irritating, and impossible-to-put-out-of-my-mind Dr. Benjamin Ellis." I bury my face in my hands. "What am I going to do?"

For once, Winnie doesn't say a word. Instead, she wraps her free arm around my shoulder and pulls me close to the love that's multiplied in her one hundred-fold since she gave her heart away.

CHAPTER TEN

ARIA AND I RACE through the airport, each of us dragging a wheeled carry-on. "If we miss our connection in Dallas, I don't know if we'll make your one o'clock lesson in New York."

"It's not Ira's daughter's fault she was late getting to the ranch to babysit Ira and Teeny," Aria huffs. "Ira says sometimes goats get out and Esther doesn't run as fast as she used to."

Picturing a stout woman with short legs chasing goats should strike me as funny, but it doesn't. "Esther doesn't have goats."

"Geez, Mom." Aria throw me an eyeroll. "It's Ira's way of saying that sometimes life gets in the way."

"Oh, right." Capturing a solution to my financial dilemma feels as futile as chasing goats. "Sorry for snapping, Ari." I steer her around a woman pushing a stroller. "Guess I'm nervous."

"Why are *you* nervous?" Aria's stride matches mine. "I'm the one who's been assigned to play for *the* Julian Marshall. Do you know who he is?"

"Yes, I picked him."

"You picked him?"

I pick up the pace. "Yes."

"Mom." Aria hurries after me. "Why would you pick a tutor who won a Tchaikovsky Competition and has taught master piano classes all over the world?"

"Because, he's on the pre-college selection committee and after today, Julian Marshall will know the name of Aria McCandless."

"You sound like Grandmother McCandless."

I feign a wounded heart by slapping my hand on my chest, but in truth, the accusation stings. "Say it isn't so."

"Say we don't have to stay with her while we're in New York and I'll feel better about this whole trip."

I stop in the middle of the concourse and clamp both hands on her shoulders. "Once you get accepted into Juilliard, you'll have to fly to New York on Friday nights so that you can be in class by eight on Saturday mornings. The classes run so late on Saturday, you won't be able to fly back to Texas until Sunday morning." I weigh the wisdom of confessing to how low I've stooped, but after breaking her heart by keeping her in the dark about my own family secrets, I've sworn to tell her as much truth as I believe she can handle. "Your Grandmother McCandless has graciously agreed to let you stay with her."

"What's going to happen to my band if I'm not there on Saturdays?"

"I'll fill in for you."

"Geez, Mom." Aria rolls her eyes. "Are you trying to completely kill my music career?"

New York City is surprisingly warm for late September. I peel off my sweater as I wait for the receptionist in the pre-college administration office to acknowledge our presence.

I chose this particular Saturday for two reasons.

One, we needed a three-day weekend to really explore the city. Missing the teacher in-service day scheduled for Monday seemed like the perfect answer.

Two, I want Aria to experience as many of Juilliard's Saturday pre-college classes as possible. With a little extra finessing, I managed to gain permission for us to visit the afternoon dance and vocal sessions after her private lesson. Weekends in the Big Apple will be a big change from what she's grown to love about the slow pace of rural Addisonville. I want her prepared for what she's getting into.

The receptionist hands us a campus map. "Mr. Marshall's free period starts in five minutes." She sends us off to locate the piano instructor on our own.

We pass more large and small performance spaces than I can count. Most of them are packed with dance, theater, or orchestral students hard at work behind the glass. Every hall is abuzz with the music that slips beneath the closed doors of classrooms and practice rooms.

I love how all the music comes together in a dissonant and yet strangely connected cacophony. In an unexpected way, the sound reminds me of sitting on Momma's porch late at night and listening to wildlife serenades. Guilt stabs my gut. My mother had a stack of reasons for being reluctant to let the ranch go. Until now, it's never occurred to me how closely the melodies of nature mimicked the music of her dream of Juilliard. If I let myself dwell on the gleam in Sam Sparks' eyes when I took my bottom-line number to his office, I won't be able to go through with any of this.

"I think this is Mr. Marshall's practice room." I point to a closed door with a small rectangular window. A flawless piano concerto fingers its way into the hall. I peek through the glass. "He looks nice." A balding man with a fringe of white hair is playing one of the two shiny black baby grands. "Ready?"

Aria backs away. "Maybe this is a bad idea."

"I don't think he's going to eat you, Ari."

"Geez, Mom." She rolls her eyes and shifts her backpack.

I snag Aria's arm. "Don't do this for me," I say. "Do it for you." I smile. "No matter what happens, I want you to know that at least you tried. Okay?"

Aria's blue eyes search mine. "I can't."

"You can." I hope she can see how much I believe in her. I reach around my neck and unhook the treble clef necklace Momma gave me. "Wear this." I fasten the silver chain around her neck and kiss her cheek. "I love you."

She gives me a faint nod. "Love you."

I knock and the man waves us in. He stands and offers Aria his hand. "Ah, you must be Aria. All the way from Texas."

"Yes," she says.

Feeling the need to fill in for her lack of excitement, I add, "We left quite early this morning."

"Well, Aria," he motions for her to take a seat at the other piano. "If you're as musical as your name, we shall have a lovely time." His heavy-lidded eyes and grandfatherly-like manner put us at ease. "Did you pass the coffee shop, Mrs. McCandless?"

"I did."

"Aria will meet you there in an hour and fifteen minutes." His nod toward the door is my cue to leave.

"I was hoping to listen in."

"The less distraction for the student, the better," he says firmly.

The practice room door flies open. "Julian. My accompanist called in sick at the last moment." The top-heavy red head stops in her tracks and looks us over. "Drat. I was hoping to grab you to accompany a private lesson, but I see that you have a student."

"Sorry, Cori." Mr. Marshall pushes his glasses into place. "Perhaps you can find someone in the faculty lounge."

"Already tried that." She wrings her hands. "I can accompany the young man myself, but I always feel I've short-changed a vocal student when they can't have my full attention."

"Mom plays," Aria volunteers.

"Really?" Cori assesses me with such intense curiosity that I inch my fingers under the sweater draped over my arm.

"Quite well," Aria adds, suddenly very chatty. "She teaches music at my school."

My daughter's unusual expression of pride in me is the only thing keeping me from looking for an exit. "Ari, I'm sure Miss . . . "

"Evant." The gregarious woman cocks her head then offers me a hearty and confident handshake. "Would you mind? It's nothing tricky. Just a few warm-up scales and a bit of an aria."

"Opera?" I'm stumbling all over myself trying to think of good excuse to find the coffee shop. "I don't think—"

"You sight read, right?" Her question is more of an assumption. "Ms. . . .?"

I nod. "McCandless."

"Perfect," she concludes as if my commitment to helping her is settled. "The little fellow has flown here all the way from Nebraska for a private lesson and now he shan't go home disappointed."

"Go on, Mom. I'll meet you at the coffee shop after my lesson." Aria is exceptionally pleased with herself. "About an hour, right, Mr. Marshall?"

"Quite right, Ms. McCandless." Mr. Marshall's slight grin seems to indicate his pleasure at Aria's display of ingenuity and bullheadedness. Obviously, he's never lived with such a strong-willed child on a daily basis.

"Good, it's all settled." Ms. Evant takes my elbow. "We're on the next floor, Ms. McCandless."

Ms. Evant chatters constantly, pointing out classrooms, practice rooms, and three additional performance venues of varying sizes.

"Tuition dollars at work." She ushers me into a room bright with natural light and big enough to accommodate the Mormon Tabernacle Choir. "Here we are."

A thin young man with an explosion of sandy blond hair stands in front of a floor-to-ceiling bank of windows that overlook New York City. This inviting learning space is a far cry from the creaky stage, old piano, and musty curtains of the Addisonville ISD's small auditorium.

"Wow," is all I can think to say.

"We're back in business, Toby." Ms. Evant announces to the pensive young man and his two very anxious parents. After quick introductions, Ms. Evant sends the parents to the coffee shop and me to the $70,000 Steinway.

"Key of C, please, Ms. McCandless." She turns to Toby. "Sing, dear boy."

On his first run, Toby's nerves get the better of him. Ms. Evant encourages him to take a drink of water. While Toby works to catch his breath, Ms. Evant corrects his body posture, teaches him a better breathing technique, and gently coaxes him out of his shell. I watch, listen, and mentally take notes from this very gifted teacher. Toby sets his feet a shoulder's width apart and inhales deeply. His nod to me indicates he's ready to give it another go. This time he sets loose a run of exquisite tenor notes. Within minutes, Ms. Evant has her smiling student warmed up and ready to move on to the serious work of performing the operatic piece he has prepared.

Toby pulls sheet music from his backpack.

"Lensky?" Ms. Evant's brows raise. "Young man, Lensky is a sing-at-your-own-risk selection on the best of days. Since you've not brought your own pianist, it could be disastrous."

"Your letter said accompaniment came with the private lesson." Toby may have picked the wrong piece of music but his unwillingness to back down impresses Ms. Evant with the knowledge that she has not picked the wrong boy in which to invest.

"Lensky, it is." Ms. Evant turns to me. "I apologize Ms. McCandless. The score to this particular aria is a tough sight-read and an even tougher story to interpret." Ms. Evant drops several battered sheets against the piano's music desk. "I wish you both luck."

I palm the wrinkles from the unfamiliar score. The problem will not lie in my ability to quickly interpret the printed page; Momma has seen to that. My struggle will be convincing my fingers to execute each and every note in a way that best supports Toby's interpretation. A quick glance at the first few measures sets the tone and rhythm of the piece in my head. From there, I can see and hear the song's story. I hope my take matches the thoughts and goals of the young opera singer.

Praying what little experience I've gained from accompanying my own students has trained me to listen, read, and play at the same time, I place my fingers on the keys and wade in. Toby joins with impeccable timing and tone. Set to adjust where necessary, my gaze darts from the music to the boy. Allowing my breathing to mesh with his quickly puts us in perfect sync. The further we go into the piece, the harder it is to know if he's following me or if I'm following him. My eyes return to the music, and I'm so swept away I don't need to look up again until the selection is finished.

Ms. Evant is beaming. And not at Toby. But at me. "Beautifully done."

I blush and look at my watch. "I need to check on my daughter."

"Please stay, Ms. McCandless." She gives Toby a thorough and encouraging review, then sends him from the room with a light, hopeful skip in his step. "So, what do you think?" she asks me.

That you're the kind of teacher I want to be when I grow up.

I push back from the piano. "I think you've found a very talented new tenor."

"Ms. McCandless." Cori catches my arm. "I think I've also found an amazing accompanist."

I shake my head. "You're the amazing one. Watching you pull the very best out of that frightened yet talented student was . . . inspiring. I want to teach with eyes and ears that search for the potential in each of my students and with the wisdom to know which tools to offer that will help them soar."

Understanding twinkles in Ms. Evant's eyes. "I suspect you already do."

I hand her the sheet music Toby left behind. "I'm a second-year teacher in a small, third-rate rural school. I've got a lot to learn."

"And yet, your daughter somehow secured a live piano audition." Her eyes narrow. "Where did *you* train, Ms. McCandless?"

"With my mother."

Ms. Evant's brows raise in pleasure. "Then I must meet this extraordinary teacher."

"She . . . died." The word sticks in my throat. "Terrified of everything in the end . . . even her beloved piano."

"I'm sorry. That must have been difficult."

"Still is," I confess. "The only thing my mother wanted more than a shot at a premiere musical education for herself was for her granddaughter to have that opportunity."

"You know, anyone can play from an open score, but it is truly a gifted pianist who can tell a story with the music. Especially, when one's attention is diverted by the demands of collaborating with an unknown partner," Ms. Evant says. "We're always looking for someone of your caliber."

"I don't have the credentials."

"Talent always trumps credentials, Ms. McCandless."

CHAPTER ELEVEN

TEENY DIED WHILE ARIA and I were busy making quite the impression at Juilliard.

"Ira is a wreck," Winnie tells me in her teary voicemail. "Esther's here, but Beauregard and I will stay until you can get home."

I drop the phone in my lap. The ability to make sense of this unexpected news deserts me.

"Mom?" Aria's voice cuts through the traffic noise as we wait for our Uber ride outside the school. "What's happened?"

"It's Teeny." I look into Aria's devastated eyes and can think of nothing more to say.

Aria's the one who springs into action. She cancels our dinner plans with Grandmother McCandless. She's mature enough to express a little sympathy when her grandmother complains about how disappointed she is to have to cancel reservations at her club, but when the old woman begins to say ugly things about the consequences of running a geriatric home, Aria hangs up.

My ex's mother's lack of regard for my daughter's feelings inflames my determination to catch the earliest flight home. It also forces me to reassess the wisdom of letting any McCandless ever spend time alone with my daughter.

I'm not that desperate.

It's dark by the time we land in Austin. We run to the parking garage and zoom toward Addisonville. Bringing up the experience I had today doesn't seem right. Aria hasn't said more than that her lesson was okay. We make the nearly two-hour drive home in silence.

Aria reaches for my hand as the Escort bounces over the cattleguard at the Fossil Ridge Ranch entrance. "Why does it hurt so bad to lose someone?"

I squeeze her gifted fingers. "That's how love works, Ari."

Momma's two-story farmhouse is ablaze with lights. Cars crowd the drive. Friends and neighbors have rallied around the Slocum family so often these last few months you'd think I'd be used to it by now, but it's just another reminder of how much I've lost.

I park the Escort next to Itty's pickup. As I walk between our vehicles, I run my palm over the truck's hood. Cool. There's no way I can ever repay the countless things he's done to support my family. Coming to Ira's rescue is another debt I owe this generous man.

Hand in hand, Aria and I trudge up the porch steps. The aroma of casseroles and the murmur of well-meaning souls drift through the screen.

"Here they are." Winnie has Truman strapped to her chest. She opens her arms and pulls me up against her baby. "We need to talk," Winnie whispers in my ear.

"Later," I say. "I need to find Ira."

"He's on the couch."

The living room is a sea of people. Aria and I inch our way through the condolences until we find Itty sitting with his arm draped around a sobbing old man. The tender sight triggers memories of the long hours Ira and Itty spent with me in this very room as we waited on Momma to pass. I'm so grateful Teeny didn't suffer.

Compassion flickers in Itty's eyes when he sees me. He rises to his feet and opens his arms. We hug with the awkwardness of two people who don't trust themselves not to give in to how they really feel if they show physical affection.

Evan, Ember, and Brandon rush forward and surround Aria. They allow her to hug Ira then, herd her outside so that she doesn't have to hear the details.

"Ira?" Itty and I lower ourselves on either side of Ira. The dear man smells faintly of the peanut butter and birdseed he uses to build his corncob bird feeders. "I'm sorry I wasn't here."

"No," Ira grabs my hand. "Teeny had promised Sara she'd make sure you and Aria went to New York."

Teeny's loyalty to my mother brings a swell of tears to my eyes. "That explains the twenty Teeny gave me for cab fare."

Ira rubs his head. "Teeny said she was going back to bed after we got you girls off. I thought she was just moping around, thinking about how quiet it will be here on Saturdays without Aria and her band." Ira turns to Itty. "I should've called you earlier, Doc."

"Ira, Teeny's heart just gave out." Itty's comforting gaze finds mine over the top of Ira's bald head. "There's nothing any of us could have done. Nothing." His emphasis on *nothing* is meant for me. This man knows me so well that he can see the guilt I'm wearing like a winter coat. His attempt to lighten my load is both comforting and disconcerting.

"When I finally went to check on her," Ira says, refusing the hot tea his daughter offers. "Teeny was lying on top of her bedspread. Dressed in her Sunday best and with her hair fixed with one of those big bows." He swiped the tear on his cheek. "More peaceful than I've ever seen her." Ira squeezes my hand. "She and Sara are flying fossils together now."

The lump in my throat makes it impossible for me to say anything so I nod.

One by one, neighbors and friends offer their condolences then leave us to sort through our grief. Brandon and Esther put Ira to bed. Aria and I walk Ember and Evan out to the porch. I can't stand the tears that spring from Aria's eyes when I thank the Miller kids for being such good friends to my daughter.

Aria and I stand arm-in-arm as the taillights of Evan's car disappear down the lane.

"I told them how awesome Juilliard is, but I didn't tell them everything," Aria's voice is small under the big, starry sky. The sounds of the city seem so far away.

"We don't have to make any decisions tonight." I wrap my daughter in a hug. "Esther is using your room. You'll have to bunk with me."

"Want me to make up the couch for Brandon?" she asks.

"That would be great." I tuck a blonde curl behind her ear. "Mind if I sit out here for a bit?"

Aria inhales the thick night air. "Teeny may have been a Yankee, but she loved country living in the South."

"That she did."

"I'll run Itty out of the kitchen." Aria starts for the screen door, then turns. "Mom, thanks for making Teeny part of our family."

Momma's I-told-you-so rings in my head. "Nana used to say, friends are the family you choose."

"I'm glad Teeny chose us."

"Me too, sweetheart."

On the far end of the porch, the swing where Momma once sat with her arms draped around Ira and Teeny and defiantly declared them family creaks in the breeze.

I slump onto the slatted-seat and finger the rusty support chains. The oppressive heat of an Indian summer day drapes the night in an oppressive shroud, a reminder that nature does not live by man's calendar. That the seasons of life follow their own rules. Dates flipping by on a calendar age us, but they cannot rush the vibrant colors of fall. The oaks will not tarnish, and the sumac will not flame red until the first frost. Whether the first cold snap hits the Texas Hill Country in late October or mid-December is totally dependent upon the mercy of God.

I can hear the distant flow of the river. It continues to cut through Slocum land as if nothing has changed. Yet, I know to believe this soothing babble is to believe a lie. I can feel the chill of winter seeping deep into my bones. It's not the first time the river has lied to me, but if I go through with my plan, it could very well be the last.

"Coffee?" Itty's a tower of strength standing before me. "It's decaf."

"Doesn't matter." I wrap my cold hands around the warmth of the cup. "I probably won't be able to sleep much tonight anyway."

"You've had a long day."

I offer him a grateful smile. "So have you." I scoot over to make room for him on the swing. "Thanks for—"

"You know how I feel about you and your family." He leans in to kiss me, but I put up my palm to stop him.

"Itty, I have to tell you about New York."

"Okay." He drapes his arm over the back of the swing. "I've been dying to hear how it went for Aria."

"In some ways, it was a dream come true."

"I knew it!" He's so pleased, he jumps up from the swing and does a silly little dance.

"The faculty was very impressed." I wish there was a better way to tell him the rest, but there isn't. So, I just say it, "The faculty was impressed with Aria and . . . with me."

Confusion quirks his head. "With you?"

I pat the swing, and he sits. "An accompanist didn't show up for a vocal audition and Aria volunteered me to play and the opera professor was very impressed and . . . they mentioned Aria might come tuition free *if* . . . I accept a teaching position."

"For the weekends?"

I shake my head. "Full time."

Itty stiffens beside me. "You're moving to New York?"

"Nothing's been decided for sure." Does he hear the conflict cutting a path through my heart? My desire to stay here with him versus my obligation as a mother. "But, if they do make a formal offer, I have to consider it."

He drops his elbows to his knees and rubs his big palms together. "As would any good mother."

"It's the only way I can afford to give Aria her dreams."

"Are you sure it's her dream?"

"What does that mean?"

He gives a little shrug. "You've always wanted to go to Juilliard, and you love teaching music."

"The best of both worlds, right?"

We swing in silence. The night air grows heavier and heavier as I wait for Itty to mull over what all of this means. I feel like I should say something. But what? It would be a lie to deny that a little part of me has always wondered what would have happened if Momma and I had figured out a way for me to go to Juilliard. It would be a lie to say that being in the city today didn't make my heart thrum with possibilities.

"So, you'll sell the ranch?" Itty asks.

"Dreams are costly." Divulging my financial situation is a vulnerability I'm not willing to risk. "If I'm not here, it makes sense to list it."

"Sam Sparks will be happy." His comment conjures the memory Momma threatening the real estate developer with a shotgun if he ever set foot on her property again.

"New York needs doctors, Itty." I lace my invitation with the hint of how much he means to me.

Itty stands. "Addisonville needs a music teacher."

CHAPTER TWELVE

SWEAT TRICKLES DOWN MY back as I tromp across the brittle grasses of the north pasture to settle an old score. When I crest the hill, the cool breeze is another painful reminder of how quickly time passes. This is my first trip to the bluff since we buried Momma. I'd forgotten the conflicting emotions this land always evokes within me—a limitlessness as vast as the sky and insignificance as small as the fossils embedded along the river's banks.

Stopping to catch my breath, I attempt to fill my lungs. Smoke from the brush Sam Sparks is burning to clear the neighbor's pasture chokes the air. I'm so glad Momma was beyond caring when the Wootens sold their place to the greedy real estate developer. I remember how she tore into me when she thought I was trying to sell Fossil Ridge Ranch out from under her.

Hands clasping my knees, my gaze trips along the craggy ridge that snakes past the Addisonville water tower nearly ten miles to the west.

Ten miles.

I straighten and wipe my hands on my jeans. When I left for college, it was with the understanding that I would never circle back to my childhood home. Yet, there's no arguing that coming here has been good for me and for my daughter. If I hadn't taken Aria to New York, city life might have become some faraway memory. A place I missed less and less with each passing day. A place that changed me, and according to Itty, not for the better.

Anxious tremors race through my body as I approach the giant live oak that guards the bluff. So much hurt and healing has happened in the shadow of these majestic branches. It's almost a crap shoot to know what to expect today.

I make a sharp right and head to the small, family cemetery.

I'm surprised by how many weeds have sprung up through the bars of the wrought-iron fence Momma had built to keep the cattle from trampling Daddy and Caroline's graves. Before I can get close enough to say what needs to be said, I must first tackle the overgrowth obstructing the gate.

A few minutes later, my palms are bloody but the gate creaks when I push against it. Feeling like a child caught with her hand in the cookie jar, I scan the pasture to make sure I'm alone.

Convinced the coast is clear, I wipe my palms on my jeans then creep toward three side-by-side headstones. There's been so little rain this summer that a layer of yellow live oak pollen covers the epitaphs. I use the forearm of my shirt sleeve to expose the name on Momma's stone.

Sara Slocum

Wife. Mother. Teacher.

Such a simple life summary for such a complicated woman.

I drop onto the little stone bench positioned at the foot of Momma's grave. The burble of the river wearing its path through the canyon wrap me like an old coat. Fighting the suffocating sensation, I turn my attention westward toward the distant caw of a black bird. A threatening bank of storm clouds goad me into getting right to the point. I can't risk getting caught in a thunderstorm while I'm sitting under a tree on the highest land point for miles. Aria and Ira are counting on me to get this right.

Not sure how to start this conversation, I clear the clog that's been stuck in my throat for years. "Momma. It's me, Charlotte." Feeling a bit foolish talking to grave marker, I get right to the point. "Do you remember the time you told me friends are the family we choose?" Kicking myself for expecting a response, I rush on before the eeriness of this place drives my courage over the bluff. "I want to bury Teeny here. If that's okay with you."

I glance at my sister's marker. "You'll love her, Caroline." I turn my attention to Daddy's grave. "You too, Daddy."

A gusty breeze sweeps over the bluff and scatters the curled leaves the live oak dropped along with the spring pollen.

I listen for their answer, but all that echoes in the canyon is the haunting flow of the river.

"Just so you know," my voice edges up a notch. "Teeny is the last person I'm burying here."

Chapter Thirteen

I WOULD NEVER HAVE agreed to one last limeade after band practice had I known Itty was planning to analyze me and my decisions. How dare he accuse me of needing to negate every risk before committing to an action. Let him lose everyone he's ever loved and let's see how many risks he's willing to take.

I'm ashamed to admit that I countered his stinging observation with a fierce, "Letting things just happen is how accidents occur, and dreams die. I'm not going to sit on my backside because some country praise band leader believes the Lord will open the way for my daughter to go to Juilliard if I simply trust my heart."

Momma was right. Just because you can say something doesn't mean you should. I did not feel better after last night's tirade, and this morning I feel even worse about dumping my anxieties on Itty.

The first rays of the morning sun crest the bluff and strike the porch planks. The coffee cup I clutch cooled an hour ago. I've not been able to sleep since the possibility of having to move to New York pretty much shut the door on exploring a deeper relationship with the local country doctor.

It's been two weeks since Aria and I went to Juilliard. The teaching offer Ms. Evant alluded to has yet to materialize. Either the opera instructor spoke out of turn, or she did not have the authority to offer a job for me at Juilliard. Truthfully, I would be relieved if I didn't have to pull up stakes and leave a life I was just beginning to love if I had any other way to pay for Aria's tuition.

Since my teaching job is one of the best jobs in this small town, it's time I face the cold, hard truth. I have no choice but to sell Fossil Ridge Ranch.

Letting Momma's ranch go will feel like letting her go once and for all. And that's the last thing I want. Nobody's more surprised by this admission than me. Fossil Ridge Ranch felt as desolate as my mother after my sister died. I couldn't wait to leave both. When Momma's declining health forced me back to the ranch, I had every intention of performing my duty, then returning to law and life in some big city on the East Coast. Falling in love with my mother's land, her friends, her love of teaching, and her favorite doctor was not on my agenda.

Realizing I want to stay on the ranch but can't feels a lot like the same too-lit-tle-too-late efforts I made to restore my relationship with my mother.

Or is it?

I rise from the swing and toss the dregs of cold coffee over the porch railing.

There is one more thing I haven't tried. One more I-can't-believe-I'd-low-er-myself-to-this move. Like my mother, I hate to ask for help, but there's also nothing I won't do for my daughter.

Vowing to never let Itty know how well he'd pegged me, I set the cup on the porch railing and pull my phone out of the pocket of my robe. I scroll to the bottom of my Favorites' list. Itty would say I keep this man's number on my list because deleting him from my life has risks. I say, James McCandless is my daughter's father and, just maybe, he'll act like it someday.

"What do you want?" James whispered groggily.

I can hear him struggling to sit up in bed. "Did I wake you?"

"Good God, it's not even eight."

"Some of us . . . " I stop short of pointing out his poor work ethic. If I want this conversation to go like I need it to go, it's smarter to switch tactics. "Sorry about having to cancel dinner with your mother. Aria was really looking forward to seeing her."

"You blew my mom off." I can hear his half-empty scotch glass fall from his nightstand as he searches for his cigarettes.

"We had an unexpected death in the family."

"That old woman was not your family." He's obviously been talking to Aria, which our divorce settlement does not prohibit, but I'm surprised to learn that he keeps in contact with our daughter. This gives me hope.

"I didn't call to argue semantics with you, James."

"You called to see if I'd pay for Juilliard."

That he knows me so well cuts like a double-edged sword. On the one hand, I miss not being known. On the other, if he really knew me, he'd know how much his actions hurt me. "I'm calling to say I know you care about our daughter."

"Look." The clicking sound of his cigarette lighter tells me that he's using his old habit to collect his thoughts, to give himself time to think of the best way to tell me no without sounding like a jerk. "I'd give Aria the money if I thought it would make *her* happy. But here's the thing. The kid lives right under *your* nose, and you still don't know what makes her happy."

"You have no—"

"You're the one who's always been in a wad about Juilliard, not Aria. She doesn't want a classical music education."

"What are you talking about?"

"She called me when she got the live audition slot. Asked if I'd talk you out of taking her."

"No, she didn't."

"Aria wants to form her own band. Says she has a dope group together."

"A what?"

"Really, Charlotte?" he jabs. "It means she's recruited an exceptional group of musicians."

"I know that," I sputter. "I listen to them rehearse every Saturday."

"So you know that when Aria's out of high school, she plans on taking their music on the road, right?" His revelation is followed by the sound of his deep, satisfied inhalation.

I'm trying not to panic, to tell myself that what he's just told me is another one of his manipulative lies. What he claims to know about Aria has nothing to do with what my daughter and I have been planning since her first piano lesson.

"Hey, baby," a sleepy woman's voice snakes through the phone and sinks a fatal bite into the foolish notion that I could ever co-parent with this man. "Come back to bed, Jimmy."

"You know what, *Jimmy*," I say, angry tears stinging my eyes. "I'm sorry I bothered you."

CHAPTER FOURTEEN

JAZZ MUSIC DRAWS ME to the dining room. The table and chairs are shoved against the piano. Ira and Aria dance to the black vinyl disc spinning on a portable record player. The day Itty gave Aria these vintage treasures, she threw her arms around his neck and her heart into his court. She adores Itty and he adores her. It does me no good to ponder whether Itty would have made a better father than the one Aria has. Other than exchanging pleasantries the day Teeny was laid to rest on the bluff overlooking the river, Itty and I haven't spoken since he accused me of being afraid to letting anyone get close.

That was two weeks ago.

Sorting the funeral arrangements was an ordeal I hadn't bargained for when I agreed to let Teeny, a woman with no living relatives, come live with us. It took some doing, but I finally managed to wheedle burial information from Paula Jennings, the director of The Reserve. I can't blame Ms. Jennings for being reluctant to help me out. But her hard-nosed response forced me to remind her that I had not sued her or The Reserve after Momma's escape and that the statute of limitations for her facility's poor supervision of the elderly had yet to run out. Amazing how fast Paula managed to dig up the details we needed to lay to rest Ethel Marie McIlroy, a/k/a our Teeny.

Strangely enough, Teeny didn't have burial plans in place. Since I'd wisely taken Winnie's advice and had Teeny grant me power of attorney when she moved in, I was free to do as I thought best.

Ira was grateful Esther came to help him get through the funeral, but when his daughter suggested he go home with her, Ira flat out refused. He said Aria and Charlotte would be lost without him, and that he'd promised both Sara and Teeny that he would take care of us for as long as he wasn't a burden.

The conversation I've been putting off for three days can be put off no longer. I've been waiting for the right time to tell Ira and Aria that Juilliard's official job offer finally arrived. That the money and job description are both so good that I can't turn down this opportunity. The moment I accept this New York faculty position, my days in Addisonville are numbered. Juilliard's principal wants me trained and in place for the start of the January term. That means Aria and I will have to leave Texas during Thanksgiving break.

"Christmas in New York can be magical," I'd told Winnie earlier that morning when I invited her for coffee on the front porch so that I could take a practice run at breaking the news.

"The Frio after the first frost is magical," Winnie had responded glumly. "Aria is going to freak."

"Why does everyone say that?"

Winnie looked at me like I'd been living under a rock or something. "Because the kid doesn't want to go, C."

"How do you know?"

"I asked her," Winne said.

"A month of mothering experience does not an expert make," I snapped. "Why hasn't she said something to me?"

Winnie shrugged. "Doesn't want to hurt your feelings. She knows how much *you* wanted to go to Juilliard."

"I'm tired of everyone making me out to be some kind of stage mother who lives vicariously through her child." I start to storm off the porch when I suddenly realize it is my porch, for now. "Clearly, I'm the only one who believes subjecting my daughter to another life upheaval has absolutely nothing to do with me, or with what I want, and everything to do with Aria and what she wants for her future. This is for her own good."

"That's what you said about that rehab place your mother hated so badly she escaped in the middle of the night." Winnie can tell she'd hit below the belt dragging in one of my biggest regrets, so she immediately softens. "All I'm saying, C, is that Aria deserves an opportunity to weigh in when it comes to her life. Don't you agree, after all you've been through?"

Long after Winnie left, I am still stinging from her implication that I just might have become as manipulative as my mother. Pushing life choices on my daughter the same way Momma guilted me into practicing law.

I sit the tray of drinks and snacks on the dining table then reach for the record player and switch it off.

"Hey, Mom," Aria pants, the first smile on her face since Teeny died. "Ira's teaching me how to Jitterbug."

"She's a quick learner." Ira takes out a bandana and wipes sweat from the top of his head. "Almost as light on her feet as Teeny."

Ira and Aria smile at each other. It's the happiest I've seen them in weeks.

I don't relish telling them everything's about to change. "How about some cinnamon rolls?"

"Is there enough for the band?" Aria plucks up a hot roll. "They should be here any minute."

"Sure." I motion to the chairs. "I need to talk to you before you strike up the band, okay?"

Aria and Ira shoot each other wary looks.

"Do I need to give you ladies some privacy?" Ira asks.

"No, this concerns you too, Ira."

Aria picks up her cat who's wrapping himself around her ankles. "What's up, Mom?"

"I have good news." Spinning my job offer into something positive is not going to garner an honest answer so I quickly rephrase. "I mean, I have news. We can vote on whether it's good or not."

"We could use some good news around here." Ira helps himself to a roll. "This place has been kind of sad and quiet since Teeny passed."

I can't think of a better way to tell them that we're moving other than to jump in and tell them. The job offer, which includes free tuition for Aria, seems like the logical starting place. Before either of them can comment, I launch into the advantages of living in the middle of the biggest talent market in America. I quickly move on to the benefits of Aria not having to stay with her Grandmother McCandless on the weekends. Aria studies me, her brow furrowed. I'm hoping the expression is more contemplative than combative. But after being the brunt of several nasty allegations, I fear the latter. I finish up with a summation on how we can spend our Saturdays exploring museums and catching Broadway shows.

In the ensuing silence, the grandfather clock ticks like a bomb about to explode. Ira rubs his bald head. Aria strokes Fig's fur.

"Well, what do you think?" I may have gone a bit heavy on the cheeriness, but I'm not ready to have this incredible opportunity summarily dismissed. Contrary to what Itty, James, and Winnie may think, I know my daughter and I know what is best for her. I edge closer to Aria as if hovering over her will allow me to hear what's going on inside her head. "Aria?"

"Look out New York, here we come." A smile erases her frown lines. "Right, Ira?"

"You can take an old goat farmer out of the country." He swipes his bald head again. "I just hope city livin' don't take the old goat out of the farmer."

My laugh is tinged with pained relief. Their responses are everything my head has planned for.

My second-guessing heart will catch up, right?

CHAPTER FIFTEEN

FOOT TAPPING, I FLIP through a frayed magazine. The doctor's waiting room is empty and yet we've been sitting here for almost an hour. Obviously, Itty is still put out with my decision to leave Texas. Guess I can kiss the "family medical discount" goodbye.

"I've never had a flu shot." Ira crosses his arms over his chest. "Don't see why I need one now."

"New York City is very crowded." Aria continues to peck on her phone. "According to Google, older adults have lower immunity. Therefore, it's imperative you have several pairs of long underwear and are up to date on your vaccinations, especially if you want us to take you to the Macy's Thanksgiving Day parade."

Scowling, Ira gives his arm a protective rub. "It might snow. Maybe I'll just watch the show on TV."

"You said you wanted to move to New York so you could get an up-close look at those huge balloons," Aria reminds him.

"That's before I knew I was going to have to get stuck with a needle and have to wrangle these old bones into several layers of clothes. I don't even own a coat."

"Ira," I try to sound calm, but the thought of leaving this dear man has raised my heartrate. "You've gone above and beyond your promise to Momma." I close my magazine. "I don't know what we would have done without you, but maybe it's time for Aria and me to forge on alone."

Worry clouds Ira's face. "Am I too much trouble?"

"No!" Hurting his feelings is the last thing I intended. "I'm worried that you'll hate the big city, and then you'll hate me for dragging you there."

"This old dog could never hate you."

"You're not an old dog." I wrap my hand around his weathered one. "You're the grandfather Ari and I never had. We'd love for you to come with us, but we'll understand if you'd rather move in with Esther. Your daughter has always said, she'd love to have you."

"The doctor will see you now," Corina announces, standing in the doorway that leads to the exam rooms. Her summons is a relief because I'm not ready to say goodbye to another person I love.

While Corina is taking our vitals, she jabbers on about how much Ember and Evan will miss us. "Ember says she can't wait for high school graduation."

This statement jolts me from dwelling on life without Ira. My head snaps up.

Before I can ask why a ninth grader is already counting the days until she's out of high school, Aria cuts me off. "I told Em she has to come visit me."

A knowing look passes between Corina and Aria. I make a mental note to ask Aria what she knows about Ember's college plans.

"Yes, we'd love for Ember to visit," I say, trying to keep my frustration at being in the dark about exactly what my daughter is thinking or planning out of my voice. "She should tag along with Evan when he comes to New York for his second audition."

"She's already saving every penny of her pharmacy paycheck." Corina wraps my arm with a blood pressure cuff. "Evan's looking at Austin."

"What do you mean?"

"Didn't he tell you?"

"Tell me what?"

"He's not going to re-audition for NYU?"

Guilty anger swamps me. If I wasn't deserting one of my best vocal students, he wouldn't be throwing in the towel on his dreams. I shift my gaze to the escalating numbers on the blood pressure machine. "The University of Texas has an excellent music program."

"He's not going to college. He's going to work the bars, hone his performance skills, and make industry connections until Aria's out of school."

"No college?" I cut a sideways glance at my daughter who is suddenly extremely interested in something on her phone. "Waiting on Aria for what?"

"Their band." Corina loads the first syringe. "He owes all of this to you, Charlotte."

Aria turns fifty shades of red. Confirmation that my daughter has been planning her life behind my back hurts worse than the needle jab to my arm. I'm speechless.

Corina realizes she's put her foot in it again and quickly moves on to take my daughter's blood pressure. "Aria, I got Ember that horse she wanted for her birthday."

"No way!" Aria seems relieved by the change of subject. "Em didn't tell me."

"That's because she doesn't know. It's being delivered this afternoon. Y'all are my last patients. So after we finish up, if it's okay with your mom, you can ride home with me, and we can surprise her together. Sound fun?"

Aria has no choice but to ask me, so she tiptoes the question out as if I'm liable to take her head off at the shoulders. "That okay, Mom?"

The air has been sucked from my lungs. "We've got a lot to do this evening, Ari."

"It may be my last chance to ride a horse."

Corina flicks the syringe. "Don't worry, Charlotte. I'll bring her home after the girls get in a few rides." She injects my daughter with lightning speed. "There, that didn't hurt, did it?"

"Nope." Aria turns to Ira. "Really, it's not bad, Ira."

Beads of sweat glisten on Ira's bald heads. "I hate needles."

"Take some deep breaths, Ira." Corina pats his hand. "Doc wants to examine you and talk about your vaccine options before he gives you the shot."

"Why?"

"That's his policy for anyone over . . . " she pauses at Ira's scrunched face then redirects, "for anyone who's acquired so much charm."

I need to get out of here, to go someplace where I can breathe. "Ira doesn't need the shot." I gather my purse.

Ira grabs my wrist. "I want it."

"You just said you didn't," I snap.

"How else am I ever going to get to touch a Snoopy the size of a skyscraper?" He smiles. "Besides, I'd like to tell the doc goodbye, wouldn't you?"

Seeing Itty again sounds worse than getting a dozen shots in the arm.

"Okay, Ira." I sink into my chair. "But if he says you can't go, we'll have to call Esther."

"I'll get the doctor," Corina says. "Then Aria and I can head out, okay Charlotte?"

Aria's had so many disappointments in life I don't have the heart to hand her another one. I give a tiny duck of my chin. "Tomorrow's school, Ari."

"I won't stay late, I promise." Aria kisses my cheek and scrambles after Corina.

My phone dings in my purse. I pull it out. My New York realtor has sent a list of possible apartments for my immediate review. Suddenly moving seems very real. Heat flushes my body. I've heard that sometimes you can get the flu after you get a flu shot. Palm to my forehead, I check for fever even though it's only been a few minutes.

"Mr. Conner." Itty barrels into the room then pulls up short of shaking Ira's hand when he realizes that I'm sitting beside the old man. "Charlotte."

I lower my hand and turn my phone face down in my lap. "Benjamin." Our eyes lock, each of us searching the other for some sign of a breach in the wall between us.

"Are you all right?" he asks.

"It's a little warm in here," I croak.

Itty lays his palm on my forehead and fire shoots through me. "You're cool as ice."

"So I've been told." I wiggle out from under his touch.

"Saw Aria in the hall." Itty's eyes drill mine. "She said Ira's taught her how to Jitterbug to some of my old jazz albums. Says she wants me to come out to the ranch before you leave."

"The two of them something to see." I extend the invitation with no strings attached.

"I'll bring some Sonic burgers, limeades . . . and spicy mustard."

Heart ripping in two, I look down at my lap. "You don't need to go to so much trouble." I pick up my phone and try to close my heart.

"No trouble." Itty turns and opens his computer. "Well, Ira, let's pull up your records and see what it's gonna take to get you ready for big city livin'." Itty types in a couple of things. "You mind givin' us a little privacy, Charlotte?"

Ira mops his head with a bandana. "I'd like Charlotte to stay, if you don't mind, Doc."

"Your call." Itty asks Ira a few questions, listens to his heart, and checks his ears and throat. "Lookin' good, my friend."

"Can I skip the shot then?" Ira asks hopefully.

"Afraid not," Itty says. "It's going to take about two weeks after your vaccination for your immune system to produce the needed influenza antibodies."

"We're not leaving until the week of Thanksgiving." I wish I could take this shard of information back the moment I see the hurt flash in Itty's eyes.

"Plenty of time to change your mind then," Itty says to Ira with his eyes laser-focused on me.

"'Bout movin' or the shot?" Ira asks.

"Moving." Itty sits on a little black stool and rolls knee to knee with Ira. "But you don't get to change your mind about the shot, my friend."

"I heard the flu shot doesn't work in older people," Ira says.

Itty chuckles. "Aria been googling again?"

I laugh. Not because I think it's funny that Itty knows my daughter so well. I laugh to keep from crying. How could I even think of removing the influence of such a good man from Aria's life? "If it's on the Internet it must be true, right?"

"It's true the flu vaccine is usually less effective in older adults because aging immune systems tend not to respond as vigorously to the vaccine," Itty's explanation doesn't make me feel small. "I count every case of flu avoided a victory," Itty says. "because it helps seniors avoid flu complications like pneumonia."

I'm leaning in, mesmerized by the easy, confident, kind way Itty handles Ira's fears. "What are Ira's options?"

Itty rolls closer to me. "There are two influenza vaccines specifically approved for people his age."

Drawn to the edge of my chair, I clutch my purse to my chest. "Which one would you recommend?"

Itty goes over the choices with Ira, but his intense focus on me is sucking the air from the room.

"Thank you, doctor." My breath is coming in short little spurts. "Sometimes all people need is a little information to dispel myths and misunderstandings."

The heat of Itty's gaze burns my skin. "Sometimes."

Until Ira clears his throat, I hadn't realize Itty and I are staring at each, neither of us saying a word, our lips only inches apart.

"You two need some privacy?" Ira asks.

The spell, whatever foolishness it was, is broken.

"No!" Itty and I say at the same time.

Itty pushes his chair away from me and rolls to face Ira who is wearing a sly grin on his face and winking at me. "The flu shot is like choosing your path, there's always a risk of side-effects. But, in the end, it comes down to being willing to take the risk because in the long run it's what's best for you."

I know what I need. And it's not the handsome Benjamin Ellis telling me what I want. Purse pressed against the ache in my chest, I rush from the doctor's exam room.

CHAPTER SIXTEEN

I DRIVE TO THE bridge in the predawn darkness so that I can push off in the canoe at first light. I'm surprised that I needed to scrape frost from my windshield. It's only mid-October. The first frost seldom comes this early to the Hill Country. As the sky lightens, I can see that every scrub cedar, yellow river cypress, and red sumac looks as if they've been dusted with sugar. The fairyland effect will disappear quickly once the sun clears the horizon. If I'm going to close this deal for the highest dollar, I need every advantage.

Sam Sparks climbs out of his shiny new pickup. "Chilly morning." He hands me a cup of steaming coffee. "You must be serious about selling."

"We better get started." I set the coffee in the canoe. "Grab that life jacket and hop in."

He slides his arms into the bright orange vest and clips it shut. "I can help you shove off."

"So that you can deduct the price of a ruined pair of alligator boots from your bottom dollar?" I toss the paddle into the boat. "I don't think so."

Sam hops in front. I wade in until the icy current nearly swamps my rubber boots. Then I scramble into the small wooden boat, take up the single-bladed paddle, then begin to slice the swirling waters of the Frio.

Noting the real estate developer's white-knuckle grip on either side of my narrow canoe, prompts me to ask, "You afraid of water?"

"Just don't want to get my custom suit wet." He tugs at his silk tie like I should be impressed. "Where does the property line start?" Sam's attempt to make me believe he hasn't researched every inch of this property raises my antennas.

"This side of the bridge."

"How far to the bluffs via the river?"

"Depends on the water level." In silence, I drag stroke after stroke against the current of negative thoughts rushing my brain. If I'm going to get the top price I need, looking desperate won't help.

The first rays of sunlight rise over the ridge and strike the tiny shells embedded in the high walls of the limestone bluffs. The glittering treasures awaken a unique sales pitch within me.

"You know, Sam, the bluffs of Fossil Ridge Ranch offer more than incredible views." I lift the paddle and point toward the millions of fossils. "Visitors to your spa will pay good money for guided river tours. Especially if you bill the trips as adventures that travel back in time."

Sam cocks his head and smiles. "And I thought I would be the one selling you on the beauty of my plans for this land."

Relieved he's still as hungry for this property despite Momma threatening him with a loaded gun, I go against the decision I'd made not to care what he did with the ranch and ask, "What *are* your plans?"

"Combining the neighboring acreage that I already own with Fossil Ridge Ranch's water access allows for an entire river resort community." He proceeds to describe an upscale masterplan with luxury vacation cabins, a clubhouse with a negative-edge infinity pool that appears to drop water over the bluff, tubing and rafting excursion services, a nine-hole golf course, tennis courts, volleyball pits, a large event gazebo for outdoor concerts, weddings, or family reunions, even a well-staffed riding stable. "Year-round, this part of the Frio will be crawling with everything from honeymooners to senior citizens."

Stable? Aria would kill me if she knew there were finally going to be horses at Fossil Ridge Ranch.

I paddle the canoe beneath the old oak tree from which the frayed rope of our family's tire swing still hangs. Instead of the usual horrible memories I associate with this river, only good memories flood my mind. My sister's laughter echoes in the canyon. My gaze climbs the jagged rocks then hunts the ledge for my family. Three sets of toes hang over the edge. In the middle, my father stands tall. A big smile fills his face. Caroline holds Daddy's right hand. Momma, no longer frail and confused, stands to Daddy's left. Her eyes are clear. Blonde curls swirl around her fearless expression. I'm struck by how much Momma reminds me of Aria.

"Sweet Moses!" Momma yells at the top of her lungs, then grabs my father's hand and together the three of them leap from the bluff.

I pull back with a start, then immediately search the depths of the swimming hole over which we float.

"Charlotte?" Sam, who has been droning on and on, touches the death grip I have on the oar. "Are you all right?"

I'm jerked back to the quiet rippling of the river. "Just a bit overwhelmed."

"You're not thinking of changing your mind, are you?"

"I've made my decision."

"Is that regret I hear in your voice?"

"No, I'm ready to part with Fossil Ridge." But I'm not legally obligated to disclose my intention to take every beautiful memory associated with this river and leave the pain behind to sink into the fossil record. "I think you've seen enough." I turn the canoe and row for where we'd put in near the bridge.

Skimming the crystal waters, I glance behind me one last time. The footprint of where I've been on this river lasts only a few seconds and then disappears forever.

A fresh start sounds good, I suppose.

"Charlotte?" Sam's impatience jerks me like a fish on a line. "Do we have a deal?"

From his anxious expression, I see that he's the one hooked. It's my turn to play coy. "Send your bid to my realtor, and I'll compare it to the others."

CHAPTER SEVENTEEN

TREATING MYSELF TO ONE last cup of early morning coffee on the porch swing, I pull my warm-up jacket hood over my head. If fifty-two degrees feels cold, I worry that my blood may have become too thin for New York. According to the weather channel, which Ira watches like he's still a farmer dependent on the changes in the season, the highs on the East coast aren't making it out of the forties this week.

My attention darts to the small U-Haul truck sitting in the drive. It's packed with our personal items, some cooking utensils, three beds, and Momma's piano. Everything else stays with the house, per the agreement I signed with the Real Estate Investment Trust that outbid Sam Sparks by $100,000. When I asked Winnie if she and Bo were the ones behind the very aggressive and secretive offer, she admitted they'd thought about trying to squash the resort development. But once they learned this offer would give us the finances needed to pursue Aria's dreams without worrying, they decided to invest in another gas station. That's the first I'd heard about the ten stations Bo already owns between Addisonville and Austin.

"LaVera would be so proud that all those years her son helped her deliver Avon orders put a business head on his shoulders," I told Winnie while fighting back tears.

"You're that kind of mother, C."

"I want to be."

"Aria will thank you one day." My best friend gave me a big hug. "I'll be by tomorrow to see you off," she'd sniffed. "But for the record, this is the last time I'm telling you goodbye."

Nearly everyone in town has made it a point to bid us farewell.

Everyone, but Itty.

When I stopped at Penny's Pharmacy to pick up the prescriptions Itty called in for Ira, Gert Penny had to wipe her tears on the sleeve of her pharmacist white coat. My principal, Wilma Rayburn, cried when she dropped by the auditorium on my last day of class. She told me that she was going to finish out the year with a long-term music sub in case something happened, and things didn't work out for us in New York. Brandon called last night to say he's driving all the way from Hillsboro to meet Ember and Evan here this morning to say goodbye to his grandfather and give Aria one last hug.

I pick up my phone and check my messages again.

Nothing.

Not that I deserve a warm sendoff from Itty, especially after the way I slammed the door on our budding relationship, but maybe Winnie is right. I want a message from him, so I'll feel less guilty. I release a long, slow breath into the chilly air. Winnie may be partially right, but something deep inside me says I just want to know that he'll miss me as much as I'll miss him.

"Mom," Aria slips out onto the porch, Fig tucked under her arm. "Ira wants to know if you want a piece of toast."

"Ira doesn't have to wait on me."

"I told him that, but he said he likes to feel needed."

"In that case, maybe I'll let him take over the laundry once we're in New York."

Aria's smile hasn't reached her eyes since her audition and that bothers me. "Remember when Nana declared she wasn't going to iron another thing?"

"I do."

Aria's gaze drifts over Momma's rose garden. "I miss her."

"Me too." I pat the swing. "Sit with me a minute."

Aria drops onto the swing and snuggles in close. "Will you miss this place, Mom?"

Considering her question for a few moments allows me an opportunity to swallow the sadness growing in my throat. "Will I miss fence rows that always need clearing, or chickens that always need feeding, or a drafty old house that always needs painting?" I pause and ponder the life I've had here, both as a child and as an adult. "Yes, Ari. I'll miss it very much." I squeeze her knee. "What about you?"

Aria strokes Fig's fur like she needs a minute to frame what she has to say, and I brace for the worst. "Coming here has been better than I thought it would be."

"You've made some great friends here, and you'll make some more at your new school."

"But how many kids in New York City have a horse in their back yard?"

Until now, Aria hasn't said a word about Ember's horse. If Ember hadn't let it slip that she and Aria have been spending every free moment galloping around the Miller's pasture, I would still be in the dark.

"Maybe we can find a stable that offers riding lessons."

"Maybe."

Her flat response has been learned from me. I'm at expert at never rippling the emotional waters. To do what's expected, or what I think is expected, instead of what I was born to do. Well, I hate that for my daughter, and I'm going to work on correcting that training. But it will have to wait until we're settled in New York because it's too late now to back out. Yesterday, I signed the closing papers on the ranch. The real estate investment trust who bought the property was gracious enough to give us until noon today to vacate their house and land.

"I know this is hard, Ari." I swallow the doubt creeping up my throat. "In six months, I bet you'll be saying moving to New York has been better than you thought it would be."

Aria turns to the sound of vehicle coming up the lane. "Is that Uncle Burl and Aunt Virginia?"

Momma's brother and his wife have made an effort to get to know us since my visit to the bank and we've enjoyed catching up. "I was curious if Uncle Burl knew who bought us out, so I asked them to drop by."

"You think Uncle Burl bought Fossil Ridge Ranch?"

"Maybe." I shrug. "I won't know if I don't ask."

Aria scoops up Fig. "I'll tell Ira to make a new pot of coffee."

My Aunt and Uncle climb out of their new car. Uncle Burl reaches into the backseat and brings out a beautiful miniature rose bush, in full bloom despite the season.

I meet him and his wife at the top of the stairs. "You didn't have to bring anything."

"This is for Sara's grave, if you don't mind," Uncle Burl thrusts the plant at me. "I heard that the buyer agreed to leave the family plot intact."

I set the plant on the porch. "So, you're not the buyer?"

Uncle Burl shakes his head. "This place is too big and too much work for this old man. Virginia and I are retiring and moving south. If you weren't moving to New York, I would have turned the reins of the bank over to you instead of my VP."

"Me?"

"You're as smart as your mother."

I look out over the land my mother loved. A cool breeze rustles the coppery grasses. The river is low, so the crystal current is only a murmur over the limestone bed. In the distance, a couple of vultures circle a corner of the high pasture. They swoop to the ground and begin to feed. Something has died so that others could live.

Momma planted deep roots here, and I have just ripped them out. All in the name of survival. "Whether or not I'm as smart as Momma remains to be seen, Uncle Burl."

Chapter Eighteen

For the next three days, two small dogs, one Siamese cat, one nervous old man, one exceptionally quiet teenager, and one very conflicted woman vie for space in the cab of the small U-Haul. Reliving the hour before our departure has been my saving grace.

Right before we were ready to pull away from Momma's house, I squatted by Bojangles cage Ira had helped me move to the porch. I slid another slice of pear through the bars, but the pouting parrot turned his head, treating me like the traitor I feel I am.

"Listen, Bojangles," I whispered. "You're going to love your new owner nearly as much as I do. I promise."

"Mom," Aria yelled from the U-Haul cab. "Can we wait and say goodbye to Itty?" She points to the plume of dust following a familiar truck up the lane.

I can't tell you how glad I was to see him. I couldn't seem to tell him either. He got out of his truck carrying Sonic bags filled with cherry limeades and hamburgers. Aria, Itty, the cat and the dogs all piled out of the cab before I could lob the lame excuse that we needed to get on the road.

We all took a moment to enjoy one last picnic on the porch. I sat in the swing watching Itty and Aria put their heads together and delve into a deep discussion about possible jazz downloads she might have missed for the long trip.

Ira was playing fetch with his dogs when he suddenly sat down on the porch steps and began to complain of chest pains. Itty ran to his truck and got his stethoscope.

"I think it's stress, Ira," Itty said after giving Ira a thorough check over and a chance to relax. "If you change your mind and want to stay behind, I'll run you to Hillsboro."

"No, I'm ready for the Big Apple," Ira argued.

"But is the Big Apple ready for you?" Itty's eyes flicked to me, and even with the distance between us, I was thankful to have him there. "Any of you, for that matter."

My cheeks flamed. I wanted to reach up and wipe a tiny fleck of mustard from his curly beard. Instead, I wrapped my hands around the cold limeade and said, "It's going to be quite the adventure."

"I bet it will," Itty had agreed, and I wished for the hundredth time that he was going with us to see us settled.

When we finished our lunch, Itty gave Ira a hearty handshake and reassured the old man he'd continue working on expanding Bojangles' vocabulary. Itty followed us to the truck and gave Aria a big hug before she climbed in. I sat stone still behind the wheel, my heart thumping against my chest as I waited for him to come around to the driver's window.

He shoved his hands in his pockets, gave a quick nod, and said, "Safe travels, Charlotte." He took a step forward. For a moment, I thought he'd decided to pull me from the cab, kiss me, and beg me to stay. Instead, he closed my door, then gave the U-Haul a go-ahead knock.

Bouncing down the lane, my eyes kept darting to the truck's side mirrors as if, by some miracle, Itty would chase after me.

"Mom, that's our exit," Aria's panicked voice snatches me from the constant replay of Itty's poker face and drops me back in the middle of New Jersey's bumper to bumper traffic.

After a year and a half of living on a single-lane dirt road, my city navigation abilities have rusted. I nose the truck between two yellow cabs and suffer the consequence of an angry horn blast.

"Sweet Moses!" Aria shouts as my swerve into the next lane nearly catches the bumper of the car in front of us.

"Sorry," I say, but it's too late now to question my decision to live within walking distance of Juilliard. The traffic in Manhattan is horrible and the rent is high, but I want our new home to be close to my new job and Aria's new school in case Ira needs either of us. During the week, Aria will go to one of the city's best public schools. On Saturdays, until she graduates from high school, she'll attend pre-college classes at Juilliard.

After several terrifying turns onto one-way streets, Aria takes over my GPS and manages to navigate us to our new apartment building. The wheels scrape the curb as I come to a stop.

Ira rolls down the window and cranes his head out. "I never seen somethin' so tall."

"Wait 'til we take you to the top of the One World Trade Center," Aria says. "It has a hundred and four floors."

Ira pulls off his cap and rubs his head. "That's flying fossil country."

If I wasn't so tired and shaken by the traffic, I would have laughed at his reverential way of remembering his elderly friends who'd died and gone to heaven.

"Y'all stay in the truck while I go ask where we're supposed to unload." I hop out and dash to the doorman guarding two huge plate glass doors.

While I question the man wearing a red coat and white gloves, he looks past me. I cloud crosses his gaze when he connects me to the dusty U-Haul. He looks down his nose like he's being forced to speak to a country mouse. "All unloading takes place in the garage."

We have no choice but to circle the block again, which takes nearly thirty minutes. Eventually, we lumber into the underground space and find our way to the service elevators. Two hours later, the movers I hired have finished dumping our belongings in our tenth-floor apartment. I pay the two men extra to return the truck to the nearest U-Haul rental place, then stumble in with the last of our suitcases.

The small living space is a maze of boxes and bare beds.

Ira stands in the middle of the stainless-steel kitchen. "It's so . . . shiny."

I drop the suitcases. "Have you seen the view?" I take him by the elbow and lead him to the bank of floor-to-ceiling windows that make up one wall of our closet-sized living room. "What do you think?"

"I think a goat would have a hard time finding a blade of grass in all of this asphalt."

"Central Park is just a few blocks that way." I point to a tiny sliver of trees. "I wanted you to feel as close to the country as possible."

"That's real thoughtful of you." Ira rubs his bald head. "My dogs are going to need a place to do their business."

"This apartment building has a small dog-walk courtyard off the bottom floor," I say, proud that I'd thought of everything. "You have to put them on a leash and ride the elevator down, and you have to pick up after them."

"Pick up?"

"Let's pop down there now, and I'll show you where to find the little plastic bag dispenser and the poop trash can, okay?"

"Come on, Goodness and Mercy." Ira fishes two leashes from the snack bag Aria had flung on the counter. "Not used to leashing my dogs."

I'm afraid Ira learning how to walk his dogs is just the tip of the iceberg when it comes to all the city things he isn't used to. "Old dogs, new tricks, isn't that what you said?"

He runs a shaky hand over the leash clips. "Right."

On the way down, Ira and I go over the elevator buttons, the directions to the dog run, the directions back to the elevators, and our apartment number. By the time we're safely back into the apartment, Ira is completely worn out.

Aria helps me dig through the box marked bed linens. We work to make his tiny bedroom as comfortable as possible. Ira doesn't give us any grief about not doing his share, then he gratefully falls into bed without any supper.

By the end of the next day, Aria and I have whipped our little apartment into a functional space. Whipping this place into a home is going to require more than energy. It's going to require a miracle.

Chapter Nineteen

Aria, Ira, and I bundle up and spend Monday and Tuesday of Thanksgiving week elbowing our way through the crowded streets. First on my to-do list: check out the mom-and-pop grocery on the corner. The small store has an interesting array of deli meats and cheeses, plus it offers online ordering and free delivery.

"Do you cook it for us, too?" Ira asks the grumpy woman at the checkout.

Next, we take advantage of the Metropolitan Opera House's last free peek of the season. We walk through the massive lobby. Ira and Aria gawk at the chic snowflake crystal chandeliers, their mouths hanging open like two country bumpkins. We'd still be staring at the beautiful lights if Ira hadn't gotten a crick in his neck. Before we leave the Met, I talk Ira into using my phone to take a picture of me and Aria pretending to be royalty descending the grand staircase. The photo turns out blurry, but I'm hoping the photo practice will help familiarize Ira with his new phone.

On Tuesday, I take Ira and Aria to visit her high school and my workplace. I show Ira how to use the map feature on his phone. Careful to avoid slick spots on the sidewalks, we make the two turns recommended by the phone's vocal directions. In less than ten minutes, we arrive at Aria's school. The building is closed for Thanksgiving break. We have our noses plastered against the glass when a security officer motions for us to move on. From Aria's high school, I keep my phone help offerings to a minimum to test Ira's ability to lead us to Juilliard via the mapping directions on his phone. I point out street signs and landmarks in case he's more of a visual learner. Ira's managing the navigation surprisingly well, but I can tell he is overwhelmed.

"You have arrived," the voice on Ira's phone announces.

We stand in the shadow of the glass structure as Ira takes it in.

"Well, this is where the music magic happens," I say, in hopes that the huge Christmas tree in the performance arts school's glass lobby will lift the somber moods.

"Place looks real smart, Charlotte. Sara would be proud." Ira wraps an arm around my shoulder and one around Aria's shoulder. "Of both of you." He pulls us to him. "Real proud."

I blink back the sting of tears. "Thanks, Ira."

He gives me a quick nod. "Let's go get the dogs and take them to see this Central Park."

"Sure." I ask Aria to google the Dog Owner's Guide to Central Park. Ira loses the map app when he tries to plot the shortest course back to the apartment. My toes are freezing. I don't want to stay out her much longer, so I take the phone from him.

When I start to repeat the step-by-step, Ira shakes his head. "I've had enough of technology for one day. Just let me look around for something to enjoy."

"Okay, Ira." I punch in our apartment address and push the Get Directions button. Whether he's actually using the directions to navigate, he's at least hearing the directions as we take the shortest route back to the apartment.

Goodness and Mercy are excited to see us when we come through the door. Ira rests on a stool at the bar while Aria and I dress the poodles in matching sweaters.

"Want to see the park another day, Ira?"

"Seein' some unpopulated ground will be good for me." Ira slides off the stool. "Can we leave the phone at home?"

Visions of him venturing outside the building without a way of tracking him breed terror. "It fits in your coat pocket, see?" I slip the phone into one of the many zippered compartments on his jacket.

He pulls it out and lays it on the counter. "That woman's voice gets on my nerves."

I place the phone on the charger. "Okay, but when we get back, we're picking a navigation voice you like."

The walk to the nearest park entrance only takes five minutes once we leave our apartment lobby. But we nearly freeze as Aria and I pour over her phone map to get our bearings and to sort out where the dogs can and cannot be.

"Don't seem right to have all this grass." Ira points at the Great Lawn sign that forbids dogs. "And expect a dog not to be a dog."

The deeper we go into this day, the deeper the trouble I fear I'm in.

An hour wandering around in this cold is all any of us can take. We fight the wind and increasing pricks of sleet to return to our apartment.

I shake ice from my coat. "Anybody hungry?"

Ira pulls the stocking cap from his slick head. "Starving."

"Aria, please google the nearest Mexican restaurant." Once she has an address, I say, "That's not too far." Convincing everyone to trundle back into the dropping temperatures takes some work.

"We've still got a little peanut butter left in the jar." Ira plops onto our rented couch. "I'm good right here."

"Have you ever had tableside guacamole, Ira?"

"I used to carry the container to the table myself. Oleta weren't a big fan of waiting on me."

Determined to win Ira over to the benefits of big city living, I try one more time, "Come on, Ira. The night's still young."

"I'm not." He hauls himself off the couch. "But if Mexican food will make you feel like you're back in Texas, then it makes me happy."

Dinner's conversation at the expensive restaurant consists of me chattering on about our Thanksgiving-day plans and Ira and Aria wearily pushing spinach enchiladas around on their plates.

I slide my debit card back into my purse. "Food was pretty good, huh?"

Aria stuffs her arms into her coat. "It's not Tex-Mex, but we can learn to compensate."

I don't think I'll ever get used to hearing my mother's world view coming out of my daughter's mouth. "That's a start."

Wednesday morning, I stand at our living room windows. The view would be incredible if only a ray of sunlight would banish the low-hanging gray clouds. Hill Country Thanksgiving weather occasionally turned chilly at night, but the days were almost always sunny and warm enough to wade in the Frio. Memories of Caroline, me, and Momma fishing in ankle-deep water while the turkey baked tug at my heart.

I place my palm on the intricate frost pattern on the living room glass.

According to Ira's favorite weather channel, a nor'easter is predicted to hit the city about the time of the Thanksgiving parade kickoff. Ferocious wind gusts will drop the temperature into the lower 20s and ground the balloons. After what happened in 1997, skittish Parade officials no longer take chances with the huge inflatables. That year high winds crashed the Cat in the Hat balloon into a streetlamp. A piece of the lamp broke off and struck a young woman on the head. She remained in a coma for three weeks.

Ira slumped like someone let the air out of his balloon when he shared the weather report with me.

"We can still go to see the bands," I offer.

"You girls go ahead," Ira flips the channel to the news. "Too cold for my thin blood. Me and the dogs will watch the parade on TV."

"Could have stayed in Texas for that," Aria mumbles, then goes to her room and closes the door.

I spend Thanksgiving Day dealing with the cold draft seeping around the windows, the wrong cold cuts delivered from the grocery deli, and the cold-shoulder treatment from my family.

CHAPTER TWENTY

MONDAY COMES AS A welcome relief from a long weekend of juggling teen and senior emotions. I know Aria is worried about her first day at a new high school. Ira is worried about being left alone in a strange city. And I'm worried sick for all of us.

"Once I get Aria settled at school, I'll need to go check in at Juilliard." I load sheet music into my satchel while Ira slathers butter on toast. "If you feel up to a little walk in the snow, I should be home in plenty of time for us to go together to meet Aria." From the corner of my eye, I can see that Aria has stopped mid-bite and is staring at me like I've lost my mind.

"Geez, Mom. I'm not five." She tosses her crust in the trash. "It's bad enough that you're insisting on walking me in. I *don't* need you to walk me home."

"Just for today," I say. "Humor me. Please."

"Ira." Aria slips her backpack straps over her shoulders. "Talk some sense into her."

He raises his palms. "Your mom and I will wear camo and hide in the bushes. If we can find a bush in this concrete jungle."

"Thanks." I kiss Ira's cheek. "Want me to take the dogs out before we go?"

"Nah," Ira drops the butter knife into the sink. "It's slick out there. I don't want you girls rushing."

"Remember," I unplug his new cell phone from the charger. "I'd rather you didn't go far without me, but if something does happen and you needed to go somewhere, don't go anywhere without this phone." I keep the fact that it has a tracking app to myself.

"Don't know how to use it. But these streets are packed with people who have phones growing out of their ears. Surely, I can find somebody to help me." Ira wipes his hands on a towel, but when he sees the concern on my face he adds, "Don't worry, Charlotte, I told you I'd take the blasted thing, so I'll take it."

"No wonder Momma adored you, Ira." I kiss his cheek one more time then fly out the door.

The city streets have been swept clear of the Thanksgiving parade litter and the store windows decked for the Christmas holidays. The pedestrians cramming the sidewalks seem dressed in an extra measure of good cheer.

"I love New York at Christmas," I say trying to get Aria to talk. "Remember the time I brought you here to see the Nutcracker at the Ballet?"

"You tried to get Nana to come, but she wouldn't."

"I'm sorry your grandmother missed out on some important things in your life."

"I'm glad I didn't miss out on getting to know her."

Memories of Momma and Aria pounding the piano, or working a memory game, or simply rocking on the porch swing overwhelm me. I swallow hard and managed to say, "You're a lot like her you know."

"Crazy?"

"Gifted." I smile. "And stubborn."

When we arrive at Aria's school, memories of her first day at Addisonville make me rethink walking her in. She'd been adamant that day that I park in the far corner and give her a head start so that she wouldn't be seen walking into school with her mother. I wasn't trying to embarrass her then and I certainly don't want to risk embarrassing her now. But if not treating her like a child is what it will take to make her cheer up, then, as much as it will kill me, I'm going to let her handle this.

"I think I've taken care of all of your registration requirements online, so I'll just wait out here." I give her an encouraging smile. "If you need anything, you can text me and I'll come in."

Her blue eyes widen. "Really?"

I nod, my lips already turning purple. "Just remember your mother is freezing out here, so send me a text when you're squared away."

"Thanks, Mom." She pauses awkwardly, as if weighing the risk of losing this unexpected show of trust if she gave me a hug.

I don't want her to miss out on the joy of winning this inch of leash. "Remember, you only get one chance to make a good first impression, young lady." Using one of Momma's favorite quotes lightens the mood for both of us.

"See you after school," she concedes, then yanks the door open and shoots inside.

I press my nose to the glass and watch her cross the lobby and enter the school office. The lady behind the counter hands Aria a piece of paper and a stack of books, then points to a girl with beautiful olive skin. The girls nod at each other and leave the office together.

I fumble with my phone and text Aria. *Well?*

Aria shoots a text back. *Are you spying on me, Mom?*

From the bushes.

Geez, Mom. Get a life. I'm on my way to English with a girl who speaks seven languages.

The kaleidoscope worldview my daughter will gain, a view that I didn't experience until college, could bless her life . . . if she'll let it.

It's time I quiet the voice of Itty's disappointment, quit second-guessing myself, and embrace the possibility that New York is a good idea.

I pull my hood down low on my head, shoulder my own backpack, and set off for Juilliard.

Ms. Evant and Dr. Marshall extend a hearty welcome. After a brief tour of the piano performance classroom that will be mine after the Christmas break, they take me to a practice room where I'm told I'll get my feet wet by accompanying Ms. Evant's opera students for the next three weeks.

While I'm waiting for the first student to arrive, I decide to limber up my frozen fingers. I unclasp my satchel and fish out the music I'd hastily swept off Momma's piano deck and threw into a box before we moved.

Thumbing through the sheets, I come across Aria's Juilliard audition piece and stop cold.

Chopin Nocturne.

It's not the sentimentality of the music that has seized my breath, but the message penciled across the top of Chopin's nighttime prayers.

Please forgive me, Charlotte.

Written in a shaky downhill hand, there's no question these words were written by my mother. I recognize the writing as the same disoriented scrawl that had necessitated that I take over Momma's checkbook.

That she'd bent her rod-straight pride and apologized for anything is more than a surprise. It's a shock that leaps out, grabs me by the heart, and yanks me to a place I've been trying hard to put behind me. A place of disappointment that I've been trying to surrender since it became evident that Momma had slipped beyond the point of logical thought, never to return.

What exactly was she apologizing for?

For being difficult to live with those last six months? For being impossible to get close to for twenty-some years. For blaming me for my sister's death? For not being my mother when I needed her most?

I was just a child when my sister died, and my mother pushed me away. It is a hurt I carried even when I was caring for her. Until this moment, I believed I would carry a piece of that hurt for the rest of my life.

Hands shaking, I place my index finger on the P and follow the twists and turns of each letter as if I'm in third grade and my mother is teaching me cursive. With each repeat of this exercise I acquire more than proper form, I gain a new understanding. This message is more than an admission of Momma's guilt and regret. This message is meant to teach me that it is never too late to admit you've made a mistake.

Suddenly, out of nowhere, I hear Momma's voice. I look up from the hand-written message and there she is. My mother. The woman who used to bake pies, play the piano for hours, and help me search the riverbed for fossils stands beside the practice piano.

"Momma?"

She holds out her hand. "Come home, Charlotte Ann."

"Home is gone." I rise from the piano bench and offer the long-overdue apology I owe her. "I'm sorry, Momma, but I think I've made a big mistake."

Chapter Twenty-One

"Ms. McCandless?" A tall young man stares at me from the other side of the piano. "Your phone keeps ringing."

I don't know how long he's been pointing at my purse, but from the this-woman-has-lost-it look he's giving me, he's been here long enough to catch me talking to the bare wall where I foolishly believed I'd seen my dead mother.

"Thanks, Caleb." I fish my phone from my purse. The call is from Aria. "I better take this. Mind getting yourself some water?"

"Whatever." He steps out of the room.

"Mom!" Aria doesn't even allow me a chance to say hello. "When you weren't waiting for me at the school, I came home. Ira's not here. Is he with you?"

"No." My pulse leaps and pounds at my temples. "Are you sure he's not there?"

"Geez, Mom. This place is the size of a cell phone. Of course, I'm sure."

"Why are you home from school already?"

"It's nearly four. Where are you?" Her panicked voice sends my pulse out of control. "It's going to be dark soon. Want me to start looking for Ira?"

Apparently, the day was not the only thing that had gotten away from me.

"Wait for me!" I grab my music. "I'm on my way."

Aria meets me in the lobby of the apartment building. "He took his phone."

"I know." I hold up my phone. The fear within me has a tight grip on my words. "According to the tracking app he's in Central Park."

Aria's eyes widen. "Do you have a tracking app on my phone?"

"We can talk about that later." Nightmares of Aria lost in the city is the very reason I've added a tracking app to the phone she is never without as well. "It's almost dark. Ira must be terrified and nearly frozen."

We race for the park. Ten minutes later, we're deep inside the walking paths.

"There he is!" Aria shouts.

Ira's all alone, sitting on a long, ice-covered bench. Stocking cap pulled down over his ears. Two small noses protrude from inside his coat. Except for the lost look on his face, he appears to be all right.

I break into a run. "Ira!"

"There you are." The phone I bought him is in his gloved hand, but it's obvious he's not been able to figure out how to use it.

"Let's go home, Ira."

"Bbbb-aaaack to Texas?" The old man is so stiff and cold, he may not be able to walk, but it gives me comfort to know he's still has his sense of humor. "Bbbb-aaaack to where the frost melts when the sun cccc-comes up?"

I hook his arm and lift. "Call an Uber, Aria."

Once we're safely inside our apartment, I lead Ira to the couch and help him out of his coat. "How did you end up in the park, Ira?"

"The dogs wouldn't ddd-do their business on that fake grass in the ccc-court-yard." He pulls a bandana from his pocket and blows his nose. "They miss wide-open spaces."

"You too?" I ask like a lawyer who never asks a question she doesn't know the answer to.

His sheepish nod supports the desire to return home that he'd blurted out in the park.

Since the moment Momma convinced me to take in Teeny and Ira, I've lived in fear. Teeny and Ira were old. Until I spent this last year taking care of Momma, I had no experience caring for the elderly. I couldn't watch them twenty-four-seven. Something horrible was bound to happen while they were unattended. Sure enough, Teeny died while I was trying to be a good mother. And today, while I was away trying to make a good living, I lost Ira.

Thank God, he took the phone. Terror pumps through my veins then doubles at the next thought: What if the next time he decides to strike out on his own he *doesn't* take the phone?

I rub each of his hands between mine. "How long were you out there?"

"I ddd-don't know," he says. "I didn't want you to worry, so I ttt-tried to follow the landmarks and retrace my steps." His chattering teeth are giving me a headache. "I got so ttt-turned around I couldn't even ppp-pray."

"It's all right, Ira." I pull off his boots while Aria pours hot water into a basin. "I was doing enough praying for both of us."

"Mom, he's shaking."

"He's soaked clear through." I send Aria for dry clothes.

After we get Ira changed and somewhat warmed, he agrees to eat a cup of hot soup. "Let's get you to bed." I lead him to his room. "Think you can sleep?"

"For a year." He plops on the corner of his mattress. "I'm pooped."

I close Ira's bedroom door and open myself to the reality that this is not going to work.

Chapter Twenty-Two

"Have you told Ira you've called Esther?" Winnie asks when I ring her after I finally get Aria calmed down enough to go to bed.

"I'll tell him after I've bought our plane tickets and it's too late to change anything." Phone caught between my ear and shoulder, I continue to scroll through air fares and departure times on my laptop. "I hate making him unhappy."

Ira won't be the only unhappy one. Aria will miss having a grandfather figure around. And, if I'm truthful, my heart is breaking. I should never have risked letting this old man gain a foothold in my heart. Everyone I've ever loved has left me. And each time I'm forced to let go, it's like losing another part of me.

Next thing I know, Aria will leave me too, and then I'll be all alone. . . like Momma. I don't want to rattle around by myself in New York the way Momma rattled around by herself on the ranch.

I want to go home. Back to where I have roots. I want to grow old with Itty.

The realization is a kick in the gut.

"I know this is going to be hard on you and Aria, but I'm glad you're bringing Ira home." The coo of Winnie's baby boy in the background makes me long for the days when getting a good night's sleep was a bigger worry than what I would do without my precious daughter. "That'll give me a chance to talk to you on Teeny's behalf."

It takes a moment for the ramifications of what Winnie has just said to sink in. "The new owner of the Fossil Ridge Ranch won't know what hit him if he tries to move her grave."

"Your family plot is just like you left it," Winne reassures. "It's about Teeny's will."

"I don't know if she had one."

"She does."

"How do you know?"

"I'm her lawyer."

"Since when?"

"Since she walked down the road a few weeks before your mother died and asked me to help her write a new will."

"Oh." I'm struck by how much has and continues to happen in my own family every time I turn my back for even a second. "What does Teeny's *new* will have to do with me?"

"Far more than I originally thought."

"Win, you're not making sense."

"Just come by the house after you pass Ira off to Esther, and I'll explain everything, okay?"

"You make it sound like I'm trading in an old car, Win." The tears I've been holding back escape. "Giving up Ira is like giving up Momma all over."

"You've been good to Ira, and nobody knows or appreciates it more than that wonderful old man."

"He's been good to me." I swipe my cheeks. "Can I meet you at the gas station?"

"Not up to seeing what the new owner has done to your ranch?"

"It's not my ranch anymore, Win."

"Why the gas station?"

"I'll have Aria with me and . . . " I can't admit to Winnie that if I had anyone other than my ex-mother-in-law to leave my daughter with, I would. Aria's tried to hide her homesickness for my sake, but she's suffering far more than me. Subjecting my hormonal teenager to the emotional turmoil of a trip to Texas would tangle her emotions and dreams into a confusing knot. I don't want Aria to give up her dreams simply because she hurts. I know from experience that walking away from what you really want seldom works.

"Afraid Aria might grab hold of a fence post and refuse to return to New York?"

"Win, this is harder than I thought."

"Dreams usually are."

CHAPTER TWENTY-THREE

EARLY SATURDAY MORNING, WE leave the snow flurries of New York behind and touch down in the balmy seventy-two degrees of Austin, Texas. Ira and Aria have been sullen the entire trip. Usually, I would put an end to the quiet, but I'm afraid opening my mouth will free the floodgates holding back my tears. Watching me fall apart will not help those I love the most.

Once we land, I learn Esther and Brandon won't arrive in Addisonville until late afternoon. Ira will have to go with me and Aria to meet Winnie at Bo's gas station. Ira seems as happy as I am for the opportunity to stay together a few minutes longer.

Our rental car dings the station's gas attendant bell. Winnie, wearing one of her flowy skirts and balancing baby Truman on her hip, steps out of the station and greets us with big waves and smiles.

Truman seems to have added five pounds to his cheeks since we left only two weeks ago. "Let me have him, Win."

"He's a chunker." Winnie's glow as she places him in my arms makes her appear ten years younger. "Bo says Truman takes after his side of the family when it comes to eating."

As if Bo had heard his name spoken with Winnie's adoration, he wanders in from the shop. He wipes the grease from his hands then gives us all a hug. "Itty know you're here?" he whispers in my ear.

I shake my head, but the guilt of being too chicken to text Itty sticks with me. The Addisonville doctor knows me so well, I couldn't risk having him know that he was right about the grass not being greener in New York.

"Want me to run pick up some barbeque or Mexican for lunch?" Bo asks Winnie.

"Mexican!" Aria, Ira, and I say all at the same time.

Bo chuckles, "Sounds like someone's missing Texas."

"You won't believe what those Yankees think is good guacamole," Ira says.

"Speaking of Yankees, Charlotte and I need to talk about Teeny." Winnie takes Truman from me and hands him to Bo. "Mind taking the baby with you?"

Bo holds out his hands with an eager smile. "Come on, little man. Momma's got some legal business to tend to." He loads Truman into his car seat carrier as easily as he used to change out the belts on Momma's old Escort.

I can't help but covet the happiness my dear friends have found together. My thoughts jump to Itty and his implication that I was so risk adverse I'd never find joy.

"Earth to C." Winnie touches my arm, and I jump with a start. "Want to step into my office for the reading of the will?" She waves a hand over the odd assortment of chairs around the bar where the cash register sits. "Watch for grease spots."

"Aria and I can sit out in the sun," Ira offers.

"This concerns both of you as well." Winnie wrestles a thick file from Bo's desk drawer. "Teeny thought of everything." Winnie hands me a hefty stack of legal-size papers carefully held together by blue-backing paper. "Why don't you look this over, C, and then I'll try my best to answer all your questions."

I scan the initial language while listening to Ira and Aria bring Winnie up to speed on the Central Park fiasco.

Ira rubs his hatless head and says, "I don't know what I was thinking."

"You were thinking like a man who's used to roamin' wild," Winnie says. "We can't help who we were meant to be."

I'm only two pages into Teeny's Last Will and Testament when I encounter shocking news.

The gentle giant of a woman with even bigger hair bows has made Winnie the executor of her estate, but she's left her entire estate to . . . me. The provisions are loosely worded, but basically, I'm to see to Ira's comfort and care, and to Aria's education. After that, anything is permissible . . . anything is possible.

I swallow back tears. "This is sweet, unexpected, but sweet."

"Well," Winnie jams her hands on her hips. "I've never heard anyone call several million dollars sweet."

"Several million?" The document shakes in my hand. "What are you talking about?"

"Teeny was rich." Winnie's grin broadens. "Filthy rich."

"Why didn't you tell me?"

Winnie raises her palms in surrender. "I didn't know until I started collecting her assets."

"What does it mean, Mom?" Aria asks.

"It means," Winnie says with a pleased smile, "Teeny never had a family until y'all took her in, and she wanted to thank you." Winnie takes an ink pen from the cup by the cash register and scribbles something on a scrap of paper. "This is a rough estimate of the assets which I've found so far. There could be more." She slides the paper across the bar.

"This is a lot of zeros," I manage to cough out.

"I can't believe Teeny was rich?" Aria scoots to the edge of her seat. "How rich?"

"Rich enough to buy anything either of you would ever want," Winnie says.

"Even the ranch?" Aria eyes glow with hope.

"Especially the ranch." Winnie twists her long hair into a bun and stabs it in place with the ink pen. "From any one of Teeny's many bank accounts, you could offer the new owner of Fossil Ridge Ranch ten times what you were paid and not even touch the majority of holdings passed down through Teeny's polish sausage company."

Aria grabs my hand. "Let's go, Mom."

I'm still in too much shock to move. "Go where?"

"Out to the ranch."

"You want to move home?"

"Yes."

"But Juilliard is your dream."

"Juilliard *was* my dream . . . when I was five. I have a new dream now." Aria holds her phone in front of my glazed eyes. Her screensaver is the last picture I took of her, Brandon, Ember, and Evan rehearsing in Momma's old dining room. "I want to go to UT so that we can keep our band together."

"Why didn't you tell me?"

"I didn't want to disappoint you. I know how badly you want me to have classical music training."

Aria's admission is the crowbar that pries my claws free of a dream that had died within me years ago. This realization surprises me nearly as much as what I've learned about myself these last few weeks.

Being a part of the classical music community is a desire I've outgrown.

The love of music is still at my core, but the need to prove my value and worth by having a fancy musical pedigree after my name and playing concert stages around the world no longer appeals to me. I can see how God has been, and is currently, working in my life to use my gifts and talents to grow me up in a different way, a way I've always felt tragedy stole from me.

Preposterous as this seems . . . I love the new me and I want her back.

I like the woman who takes time to sit on an old porch swing with a good friend, a glass of wine, and a good conversation underscored by the songs of wild birds. I like the woman who adores the musty stage of an old auditorium, and the students who count on her to help them reach the dreams of their own. I like the woman who enjoys making out with a bearded doctor who tastes of cherry limeades and spicy mustard.

I like *me* when I'm here.

If I don't allow Aria to follow her heart, to find her own place to call home, I'm guilty of the same thing I've blamed my mother for all these years . . . guilting me into taking the place of my dead sister.

You'd think firsthand experience would have taught me that guilting a child has the potential to take them farther from you. How could I have been so blind to my repetition of the very failures of my own mother that I'd tried so desperately to avoid?

Maybe that's what Momma's message on the sheet music meant. That it's time I forgive myself for allowing guilt to guide me instead of following my passion and calling.

"Oh, sweet girl." I wrap Aria in a hug. "I want *you* to be *you*." I release my hold and look my daughter square in the eyes. "I know how exhausting trying to be someone else can be."

Aria's brows rise warily, "You're not mad?"

"From now on, we share the truth. And here's the truth." I take her beautiful face, the one that looks so like my sister, in my hands. "I don't like New York either."

Aria's mouth drops open. "You don't?"

"No, it's far too crowded," I confess. "Besides, this is home. This is where I belong, and I want to come back."

"What about Ira?"

"Ira is our family, and he should stay with us." I turn to Ira, who is swiping tears from his cheeks. "Right, Ira?"

He nods. "Promised Sara I would."

I reach for his hand. "Just promise me that you won't leave us any money."

"Done gave it all to my kids," he says with a grin.

I squeeze his hand. "Let's go home."

Aria helps me pull Ira from the chair. "But what if the new owners won't sell?"

I thump the will. "Thanks to Teeny, we can make them an offer they can't refuse."

"Does this mean I can have a horse?" Aria asks.

"A horse. A band. A family," I smile. "Let's go get our ranch back."

Winnie steps out from behind the cash register. "Maybe you should go alone, C."

"Why?"

"Well, you don't want the new owner to feel like you ganged up on him."

"Him?" My brows rise. "So, the owner is a him?"

Winnie shrugs. "That's what I've heard."

"This may be harder than I thought." My fingers fly to my neck in search of the charm my mother had given me. "Appealing to his sentimentality probably won't get me anywhere."

Aria notices my searching motion. "Here, Mom." She reaches behind her long blonde curls and frees the treble clef necklace. "Nana believed you could do anything."

Chapter Twenty-Four

THE COMBINATION OF LETTING go of old dreams and putting on Momma's necklace gives me new courage.

A cloud of caliche dust follows my speeding rental car over the river bridge. I don't slow until I see the metal cowboys who guard the gate to Fossil Ridge Ranch. I'm relieved that the new owner doesn't appear to be in a hurry to change things. Hopefully, this mystery man hasn't become so attached to my land that he can't be persuaded to sell it back.

My land.

Determination rises within me. I floor the gas pedal.

The car bounces across the cattleguard. Momma's house, with the turret still unpainted, sits atop the hill I've climbed since I was a kid. Everything looks exactly as I left it. Three hundred acres of heaven.

After pulling to a stop in front of the porch, I take a moment to reassess my game plan. Think through the arguments I Winnie suggested I make.

The sway of the empty swing catches my attention. Memories of Momma plopping herself between Teeny and Ira and declaring her friends family flood my soul. The decision to finally hear and take action to fulfill the needs of my mother changed my life. Who knew the unexpected little side benefit would be finding the family and security I'd been searching for since I was eighteen?

I've shared so many deep and meaningful conversations with Winnie on this very swing. Although she often used her counsel and wisdom like a can opener to pry the lid from my sealed heart, Winnie's happiness has taught me what can happen when you risk loving.

But, if I'm honest with myself, it's the possibility of reclaiming Itty's touch that drives me to own this swing once again. The first thing I'm going to do after I move back is make things right with the man I love.

"I'm coming for you, Benjamin Ellis," my whispered prayer conjures romantic images of storming Itty's office, then sweetening the announcement of my surprise return with Momma's words: *Please forgive me, Itty.*

Inhaling deeply, I tingle with hope. Confident I'm doing the right thing, I step out of the car.

In the time it took to drive from Bo's station to the ranch, the breeze had shifted to the north. The crisp air carries a hint of cedar and the threat of frost. Praying this change in the weather isn't a bad sign, I make my way to the porch steps. The front door is open. A whistled tune floats through the screen.

A tune I recognize. A tune that makes my heart leap.

I hurry up the steps and boldly knock on the door. Solid footsteps make their way from the kitchen. The man that appears in the hallway is the strong, sturdy man I adore.

Itty stops on the opposite side of the screen and stares at me through the little metal squares. "Hello, Charlotte."

His broad shoulders fill the doorframe. His beard is neatly trimmed. The sleeves of his flannel shirt are rolled nearly to his elbows. I search his eyes but find no clue as to how he feels about seeing me. If he's as surprised to see me as I am to see him in Momma's house, he's as cool and calm as when he delivered Winnie's baby in the church sanctuary.

"Itty?" I hate how I nearly choked on the lump my heart has made in my throat.

He slings the kitchen towel he has in his hand across his shoulder but makes no move to invite me in. "What brings you to Addisonville?"

I cross my arms and rub at the chill. "What brings *you* to my mother's house."

"I live here."

"You?"

"Yes, me."

"You bought Fossil Ridge Ranch?"

"Yes."

"*You* are the man behind the REIT offer that outbid Sam Sparks?"

"Yes."

"How?"

His expression is a mixture of triumph and compassion. "You look cold." He cracks open the screen door. "Want to come in?"

Shock at this unexpected twist in my roller-coaster relationship with Benjamin Ellis sends me scuttling back two steps. How did a small-town country doctor who practices in an abandoned strip mall outbid Sam Sparks?

"Charlotte? Comin' or not?"

Maybe I will and maybe I won't. My feet remain frozen to the porch planks as I weigh the ramifications of stepping through this door. Brushing up against the man who smells of soap and mashed potatoes will lower my defenses. And if he's changed the house in any way, I don't want to see it. But then, if he's changed the house in any way, I simply must see it.

"Sure," I say, then carefully step past him.

The smell of meat roasting in the oven reminds me of Momma's Sunday dinners. We were always starving by the time we returned home from church. Walking into a house filled with the smell of pot roast made our stomachs growl even more.

Momma would hurry around in the kitchen to finish up the meal. Caroline and I were tasked with setting the dining room table with Momma's gas station dishes. Daddy hung around the kitchen. He'd kiss Momma on the neck while reaching around her to snatch pieces of fork-tender meat. Momma would playfully slap his hand, then both would laugh.

Before Caroline died, before Daddy killed himself, before Momma lost her mind, this big old farmhouse was a home filled with laughter.

Tragedy and pain had blocked my memories of years and years of happy times.

I want those happy memories restored and I want to make a million more just like them. But there's only one way to have what I want, and it has nothing to do with getting Fossil Ridge Ranch back.

If I want to know joy, I must be willing to risk feeling pain.

I can feel Itty's eyes drinking me in as I look around. I squelch the fight or flight feeling his attention churns in my belly and allow the pleasure of his approval to calm me. Standing in the entryway I've stood in more times than I can count, I let my gaze drift to the living room.

Except for Itty's size thirteen boots by the door and a large jean jacket hanging on the coat rack, everything is exactly as I left it.

Feeling an encouraging sense of relief, my gaze travels the hall for a sweep of the dining room. Since I'd taken Momma's piano with me, I'm expecting the empty space by the bay windows. I visually move on to the dining table and my heart stops.

The old table, complete with the watermarks and dings of my youth, is set with candles, two place settings, and two wine glasses.

Obviously, not *everything* remains where I left it. Itty has moved on. Found someone else.

"Am I interrupting something?" I blurt out.

"Depends." His smile, the same dopey grin he wore after he kissed me for the first time at the Sonic, makes me want to slap him. "How long are you staying?"

The possibility of Itty loving another woman sears the truth inside me. "I won't keep you." I turn to go.

"Charlotte," Itty ensnares my arm. "Why are you here?"

"It can wait."

"I think the truth has waited long enough." His preceptive gaze storms the wall I've thrown up. He looks deep into my soul and sees me. A woman cast into a river of tragedy I did not request. A woman struggling to find her way. A woman finally willing to let go of the past and reach for a future . . . a future with no guarantees, but the future we both want.

Itty sees me for who I am and for who I can be.

The worn floor seems to rumble beneath my feet as chains break free and fall from my heart.

I take a dauntless step toward Itty. "I came to extend a buy-back offer to the new owner of my mother's ranch."

Itty takes a satisfied step toward me. "You want to buy back what you threw away?"

His terminology stings, but in my heart, I know it's true. "Is that your way of saying *I told you so?*"

He steps until we are toe to toe. He raises his hands and gently cups my face. "It's my way of saying welcome home, Charlotte."

My eyes search his for clues. "I don't understand."

"I know you better than you know yourself."

His complete acceptance of me tugs a smile from my lips. "Is that so?"

He leans in so close we share the same air. "I knew it wouldn't take you long to realize your true dream is right here." His lips lightly brush mine. "New York City is nothing more than a lovely place to honeymoon."

"Honeymoon?" I ask, barely able to breathe.

He pulls my body against his. "It's what people do after they marry the person they've loved since third grade."

"Third grade?" I repeat, rising on my toes and wrapping my arms around his neck.

"Surely you don't think I came to your mother's class every afternoon for math tutoring?" His smile is sly, like he's confessing a secret I've known all along, which deep down, I have.

"I thought maybe you were a slow learner."

His beard tickles my neck as he kisses his way to my ear. "I came because I wanted to hear you play the piano across the hall."

Eyes closed in ecstasy, I throw my head back and dare to ask, "But what about your dinner date?"

"She'll have to wait. My current negotiations will probably take years." He draws my mouth close to his. "We're both going to need our strength."

I push back. "Winnie called, didn't she?"

"Said you were comin' my way today with an offer I couldn't refuse."

I study his face. Kind, smart, full of joy and hope. Everything I've ever wanted and never thought I deserved. "So, I have to marry you to get Fossil Ridge Ranch back?"

"Think of it as a win-win." His arms wrap around me, and he lifts me from the floor, holding me against him. "You'll have your ranch, *plus* a moderately handsome, on-site doc for any and all of the geriatric strays you take in." He sets me down and kisses me long and hard.

A moan escapes me, and with its release, my last reservation flees. "Shall we have a spring wedding on the bluff?"

He lifts his head and smiles. "Did you just propose?"

"Yes," I say.

"Then I say a Christmas Eve wedding sounds even better."

Euphoric tears stream down my cheek. "Only if you promise that we will spend our honeymoon right here."

"Here?"

I hesitate to respond. I'm too wrapped up in exactly what it means to be *here*. At home. Thanks to Momma, Winnie, Bo, Ira, Teeny, Aria, my principal Mrs. Rayburn, and my beloved musician-slash-doctor the place I've avoided for years has become the place I never want to leave.

My index finger slowly explores the slope of Itty's nose, then gently moves on to trace the shape of his lips. "Here."

He nods and takes my hand gently in his. "Fossil Ridge Ranch it is."

CHAPTER TWENTY-FIVE

ON THE FIRST WARM day of spring, I play hooky from school, and Itty takes a day off from his practice.

We had our Christmas Eve wedding on the bluff overlooking the Frio. Frost had turned the river into a winter wonderland, but the cold snap ended my plans to celebrate my newfound peace with the river in the tradition of my parents. Today, I plan to pay my parents and the river the homage they both deserve.

Hand-in-hand, Itty and I hike toward the river. He's wearing a t-shirt, shorts, snake boots, and the glow of ranch life. Since the day Aria, Ira, and I moved back from New York, Ira and Itty have worked to make quite a few improvements on Fossil Ridge Ranch. Leaning fence posts have been shored up. The chicken coop has been secured. And Momma's old piano now holds a perfect tune. Aria's friends are in and out nearly every day. Winnie and Bo let us babysit little Truman so that they can have an occasional date night. And speaking of date nights, Ira has struck up a relationship with Wilma Rayburn. I've always known Ira could be a flirt—he had Momma wrapped around his little finger—but who knew my principal longed for a life outside the halls of Addisonville ISD?

Come summer, Itty is going to help me finish up the house-painting project I started nearly two years ago and we're planning to hire Raymond Leck to help us expand the rose garden, with the understanding that he's never to touch Momma's crepe myrtles.

I squeeze Itty's hand. "I think ranch life suits you, Dr. Ellis."

"I think married life suits you, Mrs. Ellis." His smile is warm as the sun on my back.

We stop by the family cemetery. I can hear the spring flow of the full river that runs beneath the bluff. Winter has nipped the wedding chrysanthemums we'd left at the four gravestones.

"Want to clean this up?" Itty asks.

"Later. I have something I want to show you." I lead him toward the same outcropping where we'd stood in jeans and boots and vowed to love each other for ever.

Overlooking the fossil-lined valley, I realize that for the first time in years, it's not the deadly current of the river I hear, but laughter. Across the river, Momma, Daddy, Caroline, and Teeny smile and wave.

Momma steps forward. "We're happy, Charlotte Ann." She blows me a kiss. "Now, it's your turn."

"Charlotte?" Itty says. "You okay?"

My mind swirls not with the memories of the past, but with hope for the future. My heart is light with the joy that comes from forgiveness . . . especially the forgiveness I've extended to myself.

I pull my husband to me. "Kiss me."

"If you insist."

I lose track of how long we kiss, but the sun has warmed my back by the time we finally come up for air.

Itty tucks a strand of hair behind my ear. "What did you want to show me, my love?"

"Momma showed my Daddy this secret view of the river." No longer needing to win my mother's forgiveness or approval, I pull my t-shirt over my head.

Itty inhales deeply, his eyes sparkling in anticipation. "I always did like your mother."

We shed our clothes. Toes hanging over the edge, I raise my treble clef necklace dangling between my bare breasts and kiss the charm. "For Momma and Daddy." I smile at Itty, this man I love, and nod.

"Ready?" I ask.

"Born ready," Itty says. "Let's do this."

"Sweet Moses!" Itty and I shout together as we jump into that river with the same joy and freedom that I've always imagined my mother and father possessed when they knew they'd found home.

Tiny fossils sparkle along the banks as I sail past and plunge into a crystal pool filled with belief in myself and in my ability to navigate life's ever-changing currents. Cool water takes my breath and strips away my past mistakes. I bob to the surface, clean and whole, the person God intended *me* to be.

I grasp Itty's hand, and I hear only music as I plunge into the river that flows through my soul.

Keep Reading

Thank you for coming along for the Charlotte Slocum's bumpy ride home. I hope the story of the Slocum women has given you courage to tackle the hurdles in your relationships. But more than that, I hope this story gives you the courage to forgive yourself. To love yourself enough to grant yourself a little grace. If you've somehow missed the first two books in the Women of Fossil Ridge Series **(FLYING FOSSILS** and **FINALLY FREE)** you can pop over to my website at **www.lynnegentry.com**.

Remember **REVIEWS** help an author so much. I love hearing what you think of my stories. Plus, when readers take the time to leave an honest review, it causes the digital book fairies to give this book the love and attention it needs to be seen and read by others. Every time you share your love of this story with your friends and leave a **REVIEW** on Amazon, this author gets to keep on writing. Thank you.

If you don't want to miss my next book, sign up for my newsletter. I promise not to blow up your inbox or share your contact info with anyone else. You'll only hear from me when I have a special treat, insider tip, or a new book to offer you. Here's the link you'll need to receive your first free gift just for signing up: **www.lynnegentry.com.**

READER BONUS

Have you met my **other** Texas family?

Leona Harper's family lives in West Texas. Readers report laughing until they cry as they zip through this heartwarming 5-book series similar to Jan Karon's Mitford series. You can start with **WALKING SHOES** and read your way through the next three books.

If you sign up for my newsletter at the end of **WALKING SHOES**, I'll gift you ACT 1 of the audio performances of this story. I spent several years traveling the country with this one-woman show. At the end of each succeeding book in the Mt. Hope series, you can collect the next audio act. Collect all three audio acts and share in the laughter with audiences around the country.

Keep reading for a sneak peak of **WALKING SHOES**.

WALKING SHOES SNEAK PEEK

CHAPTER ONE

"Living in the parsonage is not for sissies." Leona Harper's husband planted a kiss on the top of her head. "If you want to wear fancy red shoes, wear 'em, darlin'."

"Maybe I'll wait until Christmas."

"It's almost Thanksgiving. Why don't you go ahead and break them in?"

"I was fixin' to, but ..." Leona twisted her ankle in front of the mirror, imagining herself brave enough to wear trendy shoes whenever she wanted. "You don't think they might be a bit much?" She reached for the shipping box. "The bows didn't look this big on my computer screen."

"So what if they are?"

"I wouldn't dare fuel Maxine's fire."

J.D. tucked his Bible under one arm and pulled Leona to him with the other. "If Sister Maxine wants to talk, let's give her somethin' real juicy to say."

Leona loved the way this bear of a man nuzzled her neck every Sunday morning. J.D. Harper was as handsome as the day they met some thirty years ago, even with the silver streaks traipsing across his well-trained waves. Folks often guessed him a successful CEO of some major corporation rather than the pastor of a dying church in a small west Texas town.

"I can hear her now. 'Anyone who can buy new shoes doesn't need a raise.'" Leona pushed J.D. away and undid the ankle straps. "Eighteen years and we haven't even had a cost of living adjustment."

"The church provides our house."

"You know I adore living in this old parsonage, but we're not accruing a dime of equity." She buried the shoes in the box and closed the lid. "How are we ever going to be able to afford to retire?" She stashed the box next to her forgotten dreams.

"We've got equity where it counts—"

"Don't say heaven." Leona rolled her eyes at J.D.'s ability to remain slow to anger. "As long as the Board believes we're living on easy street, I don't know how we're going to make ends meet here on earth."

"The Board? Or Maxine?"

"Same thing."

"Live your life worrying about what Maxine Davis thinks, she wins." He had her, and he knew it. "Is that what you want?"

Ignoring the righteous twinkle in his eye, Leona slipped on the sensible brown flats she'd worn for the past ten years. "I hate it when you preach at me, J.D. Harper." She threaded her hand through the crook in his suit-clad arm.

"So many worries. So little time." He kissed her temple. "If it weren't for guilt trips, you wouldn't go anywhere."

"It's all we can afford." Leona scooped up the Tupperware caddie that contained her famous chicken pot pie. What good did it do to dream of exotic cruises or expensive adventures? She'd given up those dreams, along with her dreams of writing, years ago. But she'd never give up on wanting her family whole. "Let's get the Storys and go."

Sitting on the parsonage living room couch were the blue-haired twins and founding members of Mt. Hope Community Church. They waited where they waited every Sunday morning. Today, instead of their regular offering of home-made pickles, they each had a large relish tray on their lap.

"Etta May. Nola Gay. I'm fixin' to preach the Word. You girls got your amens ready?" J.D. offered Nola Gay his arm.

Nola Gay blushed, "Reverend Harper, you're such a tease."

"It's my turn to hold his arm, Sister," Etta May complained.

"Lucky for you lovely ladies, I've got two arms."

Arm-in-arm J.D. and his fan club crossed the church parking lot, trailed by the lowly pastor's wife.

J.D. opened the door to the fellowship hall. The familiar aroma of coffee and green bean casseroles assaulted Leona's nose. If only she had a nickel for every meal she'd eaten in this dingy room, maybe they could pay all their bills, save a little for retirement, and even afford the minivacation J.D. had reluctantly agreed to take when the kids came home for Thanksgiving.

"Y'all need help with those trays?" Leona asked Nola Gay.

"We may be slow, but we can still handle a few pickles," Nola Gay assured her.

"Holler if y'all need me." Leona headed for the kitchen, weaving through the scattered tables. Crock-Pots brimming with roast and carrots, or pinto beans and ham lined the counter.

While J.D. checked the overloaded power strip, Leona deposited her contri-bution for the monthly potluck scheduled to follow the morning service. She glanced at the dessert table. Maxine's coconut cake was not in its usual place. "I'm going to my seat."

"You can't avoid her forever," J.D. whispered.

It wasn't that she was afraid of the sour elder's wife; she just hadn't figured out the best way to address Maxine's latest attack on J.D.'s attempt to make the worship service a little bit more relevant, something that would help an outsider feel welcome.

Truth be known, Maxine and Howard didn't want outsiders to get comfortable on the pews of Mt. Hope Community Church. Especially anyone they considered to be "the less fortunate." With the addition of the highway bypass, the community had experienced an influx of vagrants. Most of them needed help. Howard and Maxine preferred these interlopers to just keep walking.

Why God had seen fit to park a generous man like J.D. Harper at a church where the chairman of the elder board's wife loved only two things—having the last word and adding to her list of complaints against the Harpers—was first in a list of pressing questions Leona intended to ask when she did get to heaven.

"I don't want to start a fight before church," Leona said. "It would ruin my worship and I'll be hanged if I'll let her take that too."

"That's my girl." J.D.'s gaze landed on something behind her. "Better put your game face on, Maxine's fixin' to test your resolve."

Leona turned to see Maxine prancing through the door with her coconut cake seated on a throne of beautiful cut glass and her heavy purse dangling from the crook of her arm.

"Morning, Leona!" Maxine crowed.

Leona plastered on a smile and maneuvered through the chairs. "Can I give you a hand?"

"I don't think so." Maxine pulled her cake out of reach. "Unlike that cheap Pyrex stuff you bring your little casserole in, this is an extremely expensive piece of antique glass. This pedestal has been in our family for years."

Leona knew all about the Davis glass. Every Christmas, Leona had to practically beg Maxine to let the hospitality committee use the crystal punchbowl the Davis family had donated to the church on the condition the church insure it. The job of washing the slippery thing was one Leona tried to avoid.

Leona nipped the reply coiling on her tongue and offered her best platitude, "Your cake and platter are as beautiful as ever. Oh, I forgot I promised the Storys I'd give them a hand." She smiled and quickly moved on to help the twins fussing over how many dill or sweet pickles they should put on their trays.

Leona regretted that from behind her retreat could leave the impression of her tail securely tucked between her legs. She waited until Maxine exited the fellowship hall before she headed to the sanctuary and her regular front row pew.

J.D. slid in just as Wilma Wilkerson blasted out the first note on the organ. He winked at her and began to sing.

Still stinging from her failure at repairing her relationship with Maxine, Leona inched along the wooden pew that vibrated from the force of her husband's resonant bass. Clutching the worn hymnal, she filled her lungs to capacity, tightened her diaphragm, and joined him in praise. Musical ways carried her past any earthly troubles.

Behind the large oak pulpit, song leader, Parker Kemp brought the organist and sparse crowd to a synchronized close. Blue from holding on to the last note, Leona glanced across the sanctuary aisle. Maxine Davis eyed her back with her nose wrinkled in disapproval. Leona quickly diverted her gaze.

"And the church said?" Parker flipped to his next selection.

"Amen," the Storys chimed in unison.

"Before the sermon, we'll be singing all five verses of page 156. Please stand, if it's convenient."

Solid oak pews groaned as the congregation lumbered to their feet.

Parker gave a quick nod to the organist, readying his hand for the beat. His expression morphed into that dazzling smile sure to land him the perfect wife someday.

Leona loved the Sundays this radiant young fellow led. Unlike the steady diet of first-and-third-versers, the county extension agent sang every word of every verse. Hymns that once plodded the narrow aisles danced before the Lord under Parker's direction. His ability to stir in a little spirit always gave Leona the distinct feeling rain had fallen upon her parched lawn, offering a smidgen of hope that if this congregation had a shot at resurrection, maybe she did too.

Naturally, Maxine claimed allowing such unrestrained expressions of joy during the song service might lead to who-knows-what in the sanctuary. It had cost

J.D. popularity points with the elder board, but in the end none of them had been willing to remove Parker's name from the volunteer rotation. Thank God.

The congregation fidgeted as Wilma Wilkerson attempted to prod some heft into the organ's double row of yellowed keys and squeaky pedals.

Leona used the extra time to beseech the Lord on Parker's behalf. She'd always hoped their daughter Maddie would one day consider Parker more than an irritation, but Maddie was insisting on going another direction.

Perhaps the recent arrival of Bette Bob's adorable niece was God's plan for Parker. Unlike J.D., who never did anything without praying it through for weeks, she was flexible. To prove it, she made a quick promise to the Lord that she'd do her best to connect Parker and Bette Bob's niece at today's potluck.

J.D. reached for Leona's hand and gave it a squeeze, same as he did every Sunday before he took the pulpit. Some pastors prayed. Most checked their fly. Mt. Hope's preacher always held his wife's hand during the song preceding his sermon.

Relishing her role as coworker in the Kingdom, Leona wiggled closer, her upper thigh pressed tight against her husband's. Nestled securely against J.D.'s charcoal pinstripes, Leona could hear the throaty warble of the Story sisters parked three pews back.

The blue-haired-saint sandwich had a crush on her husband, but to begrudge these seniors a little window shopping bordered on heresy.

The old girls had suffered a series of setbacks the last few months, burying several of their shriveled ranks. What would it hurt if staring at her handsome husband gave them a reason to get out of bed on Sunday mornings? Besides, Widow's Row vacancies were increasing at an alarming rate, and replacing these committed congregants seemed unlikely, given the current trend of their small town's decline.

J.D.'s familiar grip throttled Leona's errant thoughts.

She patted his hand. Her husband felt unusually clammy this chilly fall morning. Was this a new development, or something she'd missed earlier because she'd been in such a twit?

J.D. had been dragging lately. She'd just written off his exhaustion as the discouragement that hounded a man with the weight of a dying congregation on his shoulders.

What if something else was wrong? What if the elders had voted to let them go and J.D. hadn't told her? She felt her keen senses kick into overdrive. Out of the corner of her eye, she checked his coloring.

"Are you okay, J.D.?" Leona whispered.

He kept his eyes on Parker, but Leona knew he wasn't just waiting for his cue to take the stage. He slipped his arm around her trim waist, drawing her close. He whispered, "Who by worrying can add a single hour to her life?" His breath warmed the top of her color-treated head. A tingle raced through her body.

J.D. had promised her he'd take off for the entire week of Thanksgiving. He needed a break and they both needed the time to reconnect their family.

Both kids had finally agreed to come home from their universities. Leona wanted to believe David's and Maddie's hearts were softening, but she knew they'd only consented to a family gathering because it was their father's fiftieth birthday. For him, they would do anything. For her? Well, that was a prayer the Lord had yet to answer.

The song ended, but the glow lighting Parker's dark eyes did not. "You may be seated." He gathered his list and songbook and left the podium.

J.D. ascended the stage steps as if taking some faith mountain.

He removed the sermon notes tucked inside a leather-bound Bible and surveyed the crowd's upturned faces.

Leona recognized the tallying look in her husband's eyes. He would know the dismal attendance count before Deacon Tucker posted the numbers on the wooden board in the back of the sanctuary.

J.D. unbuttoned his coat, ran his hand down his tie. "Mornin', y'all." He greeted his congregation of eighteen years with the same determined expression he had his first Sunday in this pulpit. Filleting the worn pages of his Bible with a satin ribbon, he opened to the day's chosen text.

The rustle of people settling into their favorite pews rippled across the sanctuary.

The Smoots' tiny addition fussed in the back row. New born cries were rare here. Leona was grateful the Smoots had decided to stay in Mt. Hope. Other than Parker, most of the young people, including her own children, left after high school and never came back.

The sound of children was something Leona missed. She'd loved the days of diapers, sleepless nights, and planting kisses on the exquisite soft spot right below tiny earlobes.

If only dispensing love could remain that simple and teething remain a mother's biggest worry.

Leona offered a quick prayer for the fertile mother of four. Maybe the Lord would spare that young woman the mistakes of her pastor's wife.

Leona reined in her wandering focus and aimed it on the man standing before the congregation. No matter what became of her relationship with her children, she could always take comfort in the fact that at least she had J.D.

Uneasiness suddenly intruded upon her admiration. Something wasn't right. A shimmering halo circled her husband's head. Surely the unnerving effect was the result of the flickering fluorescent stage lighting. J.D. would surely lampoon her overactive imagination, but Leona couldn't resist scanning the platform.

Four dusty ficus trees and two tall-backed elders' chairs were right where Noah left them when he exited the ark.

Leona smoothed the Peter Pan collar tightening around her neck. Her hand froze at her throat, her breath trapped below her panicked grasp.

Glistening beads of sweat dripped from J.D.'s brow. He removed a monogrammed handkerchief from his pocket and mopped his notes. With a labored swipe, he dried his forehead and returned the soaked linen to his breast pocket. As he clasped the lip of the pulpit, his knuckles whitened.

Leona stood, ready to call out no matter how inappropriate, but her husband's warning gaze urged her to stay put.

J.D. cleared his throat. "There was one who was willing to die—" the pastor paused—"that you might live." A pleased smile lit his face. He placed a hand over his heart and dropped.

Get WALKING SHOES at www.lynnegentry.com and start off on another heartwarming, small-town, family saga adventure.

AUTHOR'S NOTE

I grew up in a small town with bigger than life people. I love to populate my stories with pieces and parts of these wonderful people. The story of these strong women is loosely based on my own story.

My mother was diagnosed with an aggressive breast cancer. As the disease progressed to her brain, her personality totally changed. Most days, it was as if I didn't recognize her, and she soon lost her ability to recognize me.

At the time of her illness, my mother lived seven hours away. I had two teenagers at home. Making the journey to care for her was an honor, but I was always sandwiched between the guilt of not providing enough care for her and not being home to care for my children.

If you're currently caring for an elderly person, know that I understand the difficulty you face daily. I kept a journal during those two long years. Some of the funny episodes you'll read in this series are based on my need to laugh to keep from crying.

ACKNOWLEDGEMENTS

Elisabeth ended up having to give up her home and move to a retirement center close to her daughter. While her mind was slipping, her love of life became stronger than ever. Shortly after she settled in her little assisted living apartment, she set about to bring a breath of fresh air to the other residents. She established a writer's club and a story hour and read books to visually impaired residents. She started a campaign called: Let's Chat. Made posters. Sent out fliers. Encouraged residents to band together to make management do something to improve their living conditions. She wanted the drapes replaced. Wallpaper removed and walls painted with a rosy glow in the activity room. She wanted activities other than Bingo to stimulate her mind. She wanted movie nights, benches in the courtyard. A little garden space to get her hands dirty. I'll never forget the day I came to speak at Elizabeth's little writer's club, and she introduced me to a poet Laureate and a steamy romance writer. Both were still churning out work using only old manual typewriters.

I thank Lib, Ruth, and Elizabeth for showing me how to live well and, more importantly, how to die victorious.

A special thanks to Colleen Crawford and June Sikes Houston. These women were sandwiched between caring for their mothers and their children and did it so graciously. I want to thank my life group where we regularly pray for those of us currently sandwiched between family and making tough decisions for our aging parents.

I also want to thank my critique group and Janet Johnson for giving this story their critical eyes. As always, a special thanks to my fabulous editor Gina Calvert. Your insight blesses so many.

To my family who supported me with their love and understanding during my sandwich years.

And most importantly, to God who willingly sandwiched himself between me and my tendency to become wrapped up in my own life.

ABOUT THE AUTHOR

Lynne Gentry is an actor/director turned fiction author who loves using her crazy imagination to entertain audiences with her books. Her varied works range from the highly praised time travel series (Carthage Chronicles) to a laugh-out-loud romantic comedy series (Mt. Hope Southern Adventures). She has also released a co-written medical thriller series (Agents of Mercy) with author friend Lisa Harris. Her Parables 7-session Bible study (Stories That Change Everything) is a wonderful addition to your study of God's word.

RTReviews calls Lynne Gentry a Top Pick author and one to watch. Readers say her writing is extraordinary and her stories exceptional. When Lynne is not creating enchanting new worlds, she's laughing with her family or working with her medical therapy dog.

Find out more about Lynne at **www.lynnegentry.com**.

Also by Lynne Gentry

Small Town Southern Fiction

Mt. Hope Adventures

WALKING SHOES
SHOES TO FILL
DANCING SHOES
BABY SHOES
SANTA SHOES

Women of Fossil Ridge

FLYING FOSSILS
FINALLY FREE
FIRST FROST

Medical Thrillers

MURDER ON FLIGHT 91
GHOST HEART
PORT OF ORIGIN
LETHAL OUTBREAK
DEATH TRIANGLE

Historical/Time Travel

CAVE OF THE SWIMMERS
THE LOST HEALER OF CARTHAGE
THE HEALER'S RETURN
THE HEALER'S DAUGHTER

Biblical Fiction

THE CHOICE (Coming Soon)

Bible Study

STORIES THAT CHANGE EVERYTHING

Made in the USA
Middletown, DE
19 August 2024